DEATH PLAYS
WITH FIRE

I0531115

DEATH PLAYS
WITH FIRE

Gwendolyn Southin

A Margaret Spencer Mystery

Prominence Publishing
Prominencepublishing.com

Southin, Gwendolyn
Death Plays With Fire / Gwendolyn Southin.
A Margaret Spencer Mystery
Also issued in electronic format
ISBN: 978-1-988925-52-3

PROLOGUE

When the telephone in the vestry of St. Martin's Anglican Church in Naramata rang precisely at 7:30 p.m. that Saturday in September, the organist, Karl Schultz, picked it up.

"Good evening, Anthony," he said. "Have you decided on the hymns for tomorrow's service?"

This was a weekly ritual so neither man wasted time with unnecessary pleasantries, and the conversation was over in five minutes.

Karl was not Anglican. His parents had brought him up in the no-nonsense Lutheran faith, but he so loved to play the organ that he was willing to forgive the Reverend Anthony Bicknell's unimaginative choice of hymns so he could have the privilege of playing. After replacing the receiver, he carried the list in one hand and his silver-knobbed cane in the other and walked slowly through the dimly lit church to where the organ sat in a small alcove.

Placing the cane on the nearest pew, he slid along the cold wooden seat in front of the organ. The evenings were already getting colder, he thought, though he was also aware he was feeling the cold more as he got older. Pulling out a few stops, he ran his fingers over the yellowed keys of the organ. Considering the instrument's age—it had been donated by a church in Vancouver when the affluent congregation there had invested in a new one—it had a wonderfully mellow tone. He placed the list of hymns on the seat beside him—they could wait—and began filling the church with resounding chords and trills as his fingers remembered the music he had played when he was a young man from a little Saskatchewan town studying music in the great city of Cologne. Tears trickled down his face as he played, and his mind went back to the girl he had met and loved there. Gertrude Goldberg had been taking voice lessons at the same college as Karl, and they had thought they had the whole world before them and blithely planned their future together. But Germany was rapidly changing in the mid-1930s as Hitler and Nazism came on the scene, and Karl's parents began sending him frantic letters insisting he come home. He resisted, but as the political climate got steadily worse, he had finally been forced to leave to avoid being caught up in the approaching war. His beautiful Gertrude was to follow, but she never did. After the war he had tried vainly to find her, but she and all her family had disappeared.

Karl wiped his eyes, reached for the list of hymns and began running through them, rehearsing them one by one. He was on the last one when the phone in the vestry rang again. He knew the call would be from Anthony Bicknell to change the hymns—something he was very prone to do at the last minute—and he decided to ignore it.

It was ten minutes before ten when he closed the heavy wooden vestry door behind him and began walking slowly up the short gravel path to the road. There he paused to admire the low slung moon and watch the wind gently caress the branches of the trees that lined the road, making them look like ghostly figures waving their arms at him. He shivered, wishing he had brought his warm, woolen cape with him, then set off for home.

Suddenly he came to a standstill to listen. He was sure he had heard faint voices and the splashing of oars coming from somewhere far across the lake. But who would be out on the water at this time of night? It would soon be completely dark and far too late to be fishing. Maybe lovers, he thought and sighed before hurrying on.

CHAPTER ONE

Monday, September 10, 1962

Henny Vandermeer, Girl Friday at Southby and Spencer Investigations, inserted her key into the outer door and entered the stuffy office. She put down her huge hand-made cretonne holdall and opened the windows to air the place out. Nat Southby, her senior boss, still smoked the occasional cigar when his partner, Maggie Spencer, wasn't around to catch him at it, and it was obvious from the smell that he had been working late by himself last night. Henny unwound her hand-knitted orange and green scarf, removed her felt hat with its pheasant feather tucked into the grosgrain ribbon and hung them on the wicker clothes tree along with her woolen coat. It was, after all, a week after Labour Day and time to change into her winter wardrobe, even if it was still summer warm and only rain was falling from the skies that morning.

Diving into her holdall, she pulled out a paper bag of her homemade oatmeal cookies. (It didn't matter how hard she tried, they were always just a tiny bit on the burnt side.) After she had plugged in the coffee percolator and arranged the cookies on a plate, she took the vacuum cleaner and a duster from the closet in Nat's office and began cleaning the place, hoping to have the job finished before her bosses arrived. Fortunately they were always a tad late.

Today, of course, Maggie Spencer could be excused for being late as she was leaving for a well-earned vacation to the Okanagan Valley. (Henny had an extra bag of cookies in her holdall for Maggie to take with her on the long journey.) Henny resolved to be extra kind to Mr. Nat while Maggie was gone as she knew he was going to miss her very much and would need comforting.

It was Maggie who came in first, shaking her umbrella. "Wouldn't you know it? The day I decide to leave, and it's raining cats and dogs."

Henny smiled politely. Cats and dogs? She had come a long way in her grasp of the English language but still had problems with some of the strange things her employers said. "You want coffee?" she asked.

Maggie shook her head. "I want to get on the road as soon as possible. I'm just dropping off my spare keys for Nat as he'll be looking after Emily for me." Emily, Maggie's imperious cat, only tolerated Nat, though to his disgust, the cat actually adored Harry, Maggie's estranged lawyer husband. "Is he in yet?"

As if on cue, the outer door opened and Nat walked in.

"What a day!" He struggled out of his raincoat, shook it and hung it up. "Perhaps you should wait until the rain eases off," he added worriedly.

"Don't fuss, Nat. I'll be perfectly okay. Here are the keys to the house and please be nice to Emily."

"I'm always nice," he answered, giving her his lop-sided grin. "It's the bloody cat who's not nice to me." He looked fondly at his partner. "Just be careful, okay?

MAGGIE SPENCER'S DECISION to take a vacation had started when Doctor Lewis, her GP, had prescribed a complete rest, preferably well away from the city, her family and—above all—the detective agency she shared with Nat Southby. The year had been hectic. First a tricky murder case, then the chaotic wedding of Midge, her younger daughter, followed by the birth of a second child for Barbara, the elder of her two girls, this time a beautiful little granddaughter they had named Amelia Margaret. Maggie thought she had coped pretty well with all this, considering she also had to deal with her mother-in-law who tried to interfere in both the wedding and the birth, even commanding that the baby be named Honoria after her. Luckily, Charles, the baby's father, had scotched that idea. But what had really pushed Maggie to the edge was Harry's continuing refusal to even discuss a divorce—he was still expecting her to "*come to her senses!*"

Nat had realized the doctor was right. "You could take a trip back to England to see your folks," he had suggested.

Maggie shook her head. "September is a glorious time of year in the Okanagan. I'm going to take a couple of weeks and meander through the valley, staying in B&Bs and places like that. But I do wish you'd come, too."

"Too many cases on hand," he said. "Southby and Spencer Investigations are too much in demand. I've even had to turn down a couple of cases."

"You're making me feel guilty."

Putting his arms around her, he pulled her close. "Not to worry," he said. "I'll make do with George." Just a few days earlier when she had told him of her doctor's prescription for a vacation, he had casually mentioned that George Sawasky had just taken early retirement from the city police force.

"Yes, Lucille told me," she had said. "And she's already complaining that the house isn't big enough for the two of them. Are you thinking of asking him to work in the agency?"

"Just on a part-time basis to begin with—but only if you agree. . ."

"I'm all for it! And it will ease my conscience about leaving you."

"I'll ask him then."

As it turned out, George was only too happy to accept, and Henny was also happy since George Sawasky was one of her favourite people. So an agreement had been made, and now on Monday, September 10, Maggie was starting out on her vacation with a clear conscience.

"You go and take that vacation and bring my old Maggie back to me," Nat said and then paused. "But while you're away, I want you to promise that you'll call at least every other day. You know how trouble always finds you."

"Nat, do stop worrying. I just need a few weeks of rest and recuperation. Anyway," she added, "I don't know a soul in the Okanagan, so how can I get into trouble?"

"Maggie, my darling," he said, putting his hands on her shoulders and looking her straight in the eye, "not knowing anybody doesn't mean a damned thing with you—trouble *always* finds you."

"Nat, you exaggerate." And she kissed him good-bye and set off on her holiday.

MAGGIE LOVED A good storm when she was safely inside her little house in Kitsilano, but now she cringed as yet another streak of lightning rent the sky, quickly followed by a crash of thunder that seemed to be right over her car. The wipers of her little red Morris Minor tried valiantly to keep up with the torrent of water that poured down the windshield, but it was nearly impossible for Maggie to see more than a few yards ahead.

Oscar, her mostly spaniel plus some-unknown-variety dog, nuzzled her neck from the back seat, but the next crash of thunder made him push his way frantically between the two front seats to sit as close to Maggie as possible. He was known to be a bit of a wimp when facing the unknown.

"Move over, Oscar." She pushed him away from the gear shift and onto the passenger seat. "I should have listened to Nat," she muttered as yet another truck passed and threw a wave of muddy water at her. "He did tell me to wait." But she had been so anxious to get on the road that she had taken a chance on the weather improving. It hadn't!

When the transport truck she had been following since leaving the small town of Hope suddenly indicated it was turning right, Maggie saw a way out of her dilemma. "I think that's a truck stop, Oscar!" And she followed the truck off the road and tucked her car in behind it. It was only after she stopped the car that she realized it was just a pull-off, but she reasoned she could at least wait there until the storm abated. Turning off the engine, she reached over the seat-back for her thermos of coffee and a couple of biscuits for the dog. Later, as the rain continued to beat on the roof, she leaned back in her seat to have a little nap, but as soon as she closed her eyes, her mind returned to the miserable afternoon a few weeks after Midge's wedding when she had gone to visit Harry . . .

She had walked slowly up the path to the house on Elm Street in Kerrisdale. Harry's house—she never thought of it as hers anymore—fitted perfectly with its peers on either side of the street. *Like maiden aunts,* she thought as she lifted the knocker. *All prim and proper, especially when people come to visit.*

"Ah, Margaret," Harry greeted her, smiling. "Right on time, I see." He led the way down the entrance hall to the kitchen. "I thought we'd have our coffee here—it's cozier. Take a seat. Coffee will only take a minute or two."

She sat at what had once been her usual place at the table and instantly recalled one of the last times she had

sat there. It had been the morning of her fiftieth birth-
day—March 20, 1958—and Harry had left a glossy birth-
day card beside her breakfast plate. That had been over
four years ago but she could still remember the sappy
verse printed inside it:

To my wife so thoughtful and sweet,

The girl I was lucky to meet,

By my side through the years . . .

And there had been a twenty-dollar bill tucked inside
the card.

Now she stared around the room. The shelves of the
maple hutch still held the blue Spode plates with the
matching cups hanging from hooks and the saucers neatly
aligned behind each cup. The toaster on the spotless counter was new, but for the rest of the kitchen it was as if
she'd never left.

"I guess you still like cream in your coffee?" he said,
raising the jug over her cup.

"No. I actually prefer it black." Then, seeing his stricken
look, she hastily explained, "We don't have a fridge at the
office so I've learned to drink it black and found I quite
like it."

"Oh, I see." He poured coffee into both cups and then
carefully dropped two sugar lumps into his. "You said it
was urgent that we meet." He gazed intently at her as he
stirred his coffee. "Would you like a ginger snap?" He
pushed the plate in front of her.

She took one and placed it carefully on the small plate beside her cup as she wondered how to begin. At last she blurted, "Harry, I've come to ask you for a divorce."

The words seem to hang in the air and Maggie, lifting her eyes to look directly at Harry, was shocked at the terror on his face.

"Divorce! But I thought. . .I mean. . .at Midge's wedding. . .you were right there beside me. I hoped it meant you'd had enough of working at that ridiculous job and you would be coming home to your rightful place. . ." Harry's words trailed off and he was silent for a few moments. "Even Mother thought that at last you'd come to your senses."

She kept her thoughts about her interfering mother-in-law carefully to herself before replying. "I wanted Midge's wedding to be as normal as possible, the kind of day she'd always remember happily. I'm sorry if you misunderstood my sitting next to you at the church, but Harry," she leaned over and touched his arm, "even though I have the greatest regard for you, I can never come back as your wife."

"So much for your wedding vows," he said, angrily brushing her hand from his arm. He stood up and loomed over her. "If you think for one moment that I will risk losing *my* good name and reputation by going through the divorce courts just so you can live with *that...that man*, you of all people should know me better than that."

"I know you value your good name, and I know that the only legal grounds for divorce is adultery, but Harry,

I'm willing to provide the grounds so that you can divorce me."

"Margaret, I took our marriage vows seriously—until death do us part—remember? And in case you have forgotten, you are the mother of my children, and a dirty divorce will affect their lives as well as mine. You know my answer. And now, if that's all you came for, I think it's time for you to leave."

Thinking back on that day, Maggie remembered gathering up her handbag and looking steadily at her estranged husband. "Harry," she had said at last, "I'm never coming back to you, so you might as well get on with your life. And we both know the divorce laws are going to change, and you can be sure that when they do, I will be first in line. So sooner or later your good name will be on that line, too."

As she listened to the rain pounding on the roof of her car, she wondered if Nat realized that it was Harry she was running away from and not him and the Agency. She sighed and tried to put the confrontation behind her. *I'll just shut my eyes for a while,* she told herself, but the rhythm of the rain was mesmerizing, and it was Oscar's barking and someone banging on the car window that brought her abruptly awake. A shrouded figure was peering at her through the misty glass. Thinking of all the terrible stories of muggings she'd read about in the papers, Maggie cautiously wound the window down just a little.

"I'm on my way soon," the man yelled at her over the sound of the pelting rain. He pointed to the truck ahead of her. "I saw you following me. Where you heading?"

"Penticton."

"I'm going through there. Just keep back a mite so that I can see your lights in my mirror, okay?"

"Thanks." Gratefully she wound up the window and prepared to follow.

As they drove, the rain finally began to let up, and an hour later a watery setting sun greeted her as they entered Penticton. Maggie, who was still behind the truck when its indicators showed it was turning in to a supermarket parking lot, followed right behind it. She climbed stiffly out of her car and walked over as the driver swung down to the ground. She could see now that he was comfortably middle-aged and wore a wedding ring.

"I don't think I would have made it without your help," she said, holding out her hand. "I can't thank you enough."

"That's okay-a," he said with a trace of an Italian accent. He wiped his hands on a big handkerchief before taking hers. "My name's Donato. That's a bitch of a road when it rains or snows. Are you staying in Penticton?"

"Yes. I'm on vacation."

"Have you got a place to stay?"

"Not yet. I. . ."

"Have you ever been to Naramata?"

"No. Where is it?"

"Just nine or ten miles north of here on the east side of Okanagan Lake. My wife's cousin has a farmhouse and orchard there. Beautiful place! They take paying guests. You'll love it."

"Sounds great, but I'm pretty well done in and too tired to travel much farther."

"It's not far. Not far. Here, I draw you a map." He hauled out a grubby notebook, sketched out a map, then tore out the page and handed it to her. "And I call her from the store here and tell her to expect you."

CHAPTER TWO

"I hope you don't mind using Maggie's office." Nat Southby walked over to the window and pulled up the blind. "It has the same view over Broadway that mine does."

"Are you sure she won't mind?" George Sawasky stood behind Maggie's very tidy desk and placed his briefcase on the fresh blotter before pulling out the comfortable chair and sitting down. "I must say it beats the cramped cubby-hole I had at the station."

"Maggie's all right with this. She understands you need a place to work." Nat paused, turned away from the window and faced George across the desk. "Of course, if you decide you like working for the Agency. . ." he paused, "we'll set you up with your own desk."

George glanced into the main office where Henny was typing a report, then he whispered, "You're not thinking of me sharing with Henny, I hope." He could see an endless line of burnt cookies coming his way from Nat's eccentric receptionist.

"No," Nat said and laughed. "I wouldn't dare. Come on. I'll show you what I have in mind." He led the way through Henny's domain and out into the passageway, stopping at the door next to the Agency. "The guy who leased this room has left, and the owners of the building have given me the option to take it over—but that will be up to you." Nat reached into his pocket, extracted a key and opened the door. "Anyway, you should know if you like working here by the time Maggie returns. It's a bit small," he apologized, leading the way in, "but there's room for a desk and a couple of visitor's chairs, and a small filing cabinet if you need one. The main files are in the reception area."

"It's great." George walked over to the window and peered out. "But are you sure I will earn my keep to pay for this?"

"There's plenty of work, George. In fact, I've had to turn down a couple of potential clients."

"But that's because you're shorthanded with Maggie away."

"That's partly true, but the business is really expanding and we need extra help."

"It sounds like you want me to work more than just part-time," George answered, "and I have to be honest, Nat—I'm not sure what I want to do at this stage."

"I fully understand." Nat turned and led the way back to his own office and sat down behind his desk. "Anyway, back to business. Yesterday there was a phone call for Maggie, and Henny, realizing the caller was quite distraught, put it through to me. The caller was a Mrs. Blackthorn, and she made an appointment for ten this morning." Nat glanced at his watch. "She should be here in fifteen minutes. I'd like to go over the details with you before she gets here. It's a complicated accident liability case."

George settled into the chair opposite Nat and waited for his old pal to begin. It was almost thirty years since the two men had first walked a beat together on Vancouver's Downtown East Side, and they had risen to detective at almost the same time. They had been best man at each other's weddings (Nat's marriage had ended in divorce), and although Nat had left the force ten years earlier, they had remained the best of friends. Now George had retired and they would be working together once again.

Nat opened his desk drawer and handed George a fresh pad of lined yellow paper. "As I was saying, the woman said her name was Clara Blackthorn."

At that moment Henny knocked and sailed into the room. She was wearing her favourite hand-knitted sweater—purple with orange and yellow stripes. Carefully she placed steaming cups of coffee in front of the two men. "Sorry, Mr. George," she said in her thickly Dutch-accented English, "but I don't haf any of your favourite ginger cookies today—only oatmeal. I bake tonight."

George gave Henny a beaming smile. "I look forward to them."

As Henny left the room, Nat rolled his eyes.

They'd barely started on their coffee when Henny returned. "Mrs. Clara Blackthorn is here."

"Show her in, Henny. Perhaps she would like a coffee, too."

"She say no thanks."

Both men stood up as a middle-aged matron stormed into the room.

CHAPTER THREE

From her perch near the top of the wide-angled ladder Bianca Rinaldi looked down at Maggie who was picking the Golden Delicious apples from the lower branches. "Looks like the rest of our pickers have gone for lunch," she called down, "and since my bag is full, we'll stop and have ours, too." Maggie watched her hostess placing each foot cautiously as she descended rung by rung, careful not to bounce her filled bag against the ladder and bruise the fruit. Once on the ground she headed for the nearest apple bin.

Maggie followed and watched as Bianca loosened the strings that held the fruit safely in her bag and allowed the apples to tumble very gently out into the big bin. Maggie did the same then took a deep breath to savour the heavenly apple-scented September air before walking back to where Bianca was already seated against a tree with an open picnic basket beside her. Maggie was absolutely starving, and she watched in anticipation as Bianca spread a cloth then lay out thickly buttered crusty bread, slices of cheese and ham, a bowl of grapes and a bottle of red wine. Oscar, his eyes fixed on the food, wagged his tail as he waited for the odd scrap he knew would come his way.

"You've even brought wine glasses," Maggie exclaimed. "You're spoiling me rotten."

"But you don't have to pick apples, you know. You came here for a rest, not to work."

"But I'm enjoying every minute of it. You're not going to stop me, are you? Just imagine if I hadn't met your life-saver cousin." And she smiled as she thought back to that chance meeting with the truck driver a week earlier. She was feeling more relaxed than she had in years. Her days were spent helping with the apple picking or taking Oscar for long walks beside Okanagan Lake or driving into Penticton to shop. And, as promised, she had dutifully phoned Nat every other day to let him know how she was doing.

Maggie had never been to Italy, but she had envisioned Italian women as dark-skinned with black hair and, as they got older, becoming plump from all the pasta they ate. But Bianca Rinaldi was tall and fair-skinned, and her hair was light brown with reddish tints. She estimated that Bianca must be in her late thirties. She was a devoted wife and mother and a wonderful cook. However, Alonso, Bianca's husband, did fit the stereotype—medium height, dark, very handsome, good-natured and still madly in love with his wife who ruled him with a firm hand.

"However did you manage to find this beautiful place?" Maggie asked, reaching for a handful of grapes.

"Long story," Bianca answered in her softly accented English. She leaned forward to refill Maggie's glass. "It was terrible after the war, and my husband's family vineyard was in a very sad state. His parents and his elder brother were struggling to get it back into production, but there was no way it could support us, too."

"So you were married by then?"

Bianca nodded. "Just before the war ended and soon after Alonso was released from the military. And then I found I was pregnant with Lorenzo. We stayed with my parents until our son was born. It was very hard times." She shrugged. "Alonso did odd jobs where he could find them. Then his cousin Elizabetta, Donato's wife, wrote and told us about Canada and the beautiful Okanagan. So we applied."

"And you were accepted. . ."

"Yes, eventually, but we had a long wait. At first we worked in other people's orchards, saving our money, and then we found this little bit of heaven." She smiled as she got to her feet.

"It must've been wonderful for you." Maggie paused then said, "I hope you don't mind me asking, but you haven't been in this country that long and yet your English is so very good. . ."

Bianca laughed. "My mother was English. She was young and adventuresome, and she came to Italy with friends in the so-called roaring twenties."

"And she met your father, fell in love and never went home again," Maggie said with a grin.

"So I grew up with both languages."

"But what about when the war began? Was she in danger. . .you know, being English?"

Bianca nodded. "At the beginning my grandparents wanted her to return to England, but she wouldn't leave my papa. She had a few close calls because of her fair colouring, but luckily our village was small and was mostly bypassed by the hated Germans. But I can remember the tension and the worry that someone would feel it was their duty to tell the authorities."

"How terrible for you all. Thank God your family came through it safely."

Bianca nodded in agreement as she replaced the plates and glasses in the basket. "Yes, we were very lucky," she said. "Ah, I see my pickers are heading back to work." She stood up and waved to the two men who had stopped under a tree to light cigarettes. "Mateo! Rafael!" she called, and they turned, threw their cigarettes down, ground them out in the sandy soil and started toward her. They were quite swarthy men and not very tall, and Maggie realized that they must be the two pickers that Bianca had told her came from Central America every year around this time. Sometimes they stayed as much as a few weeks, usually when the Rinaldis were taking off the last of their peach crop, but this year they were more than welcome as the summer had been scorching, and when they had arrived a week earlier, the Golden Delicious apples had been ready before all the peaches had been taken off.

Now as the men came closer, Bianca called, "If you're finished that row, Alonso wants you to work with him on the last of the peaches." It was obvious they didn't understand, and while they stopped to confer with one another, Bianca turned to Maggie to say, "There's a fruit stand in Penticton that always takes our late peaches." Then beckoning the two men closer, she began explaining with gestures and pidgin English that they were to work with Alonso for the afternoon, but their eyes kept straying to Maggie. "Oh," said Bianca, "this is Maggie Spencer. She's here for a holiday." Then she added, "She's a detective."

"Detective?" Mateo said anxiously and turned to say something in Spanish to his partner.

Bianca laughed and said the word in Italian—"*Investigatore*"—in case that would have more meaning for them. "I think they are impressed," she said and then went back to explaining to them that they were to work with Alonso.

Finally they said, "Si," several times, nodded to indicate they understood her orders and set off toward the peach section of the orchard, but they seemed worried and kept glancing back at the two women.

"I don't think they have lady detectives in their country," Bianca said, amused.

"It's strange," Maggie said, "they would come all this way to pick fruit for just a few weeks."

"Oh, we have many migrant workers in the valley," Bianca said. "They work their way up the West Coast—picking oranges in California and strawberries and beans in Washington State—and then they cross the border to pick fruit here. When the picking season ends, they go home for the winter."

"Do they camp out?"

"In some places I think so, but when they're here, Mateo and Rafael always stay in the pickers' cabins on Major Stroud's orchard—it's not far from here, on the way in to Penticton. . ." she waved an arm in a generally southern direction, ". . . and they work for him, too. Now why don't you go back to the house and have a rest? I'm about finished for the day and then I have to go and pick up supplies from the village."

"At least let me take this back to the house," Maggie said, bending to swoop up the picnic basket. "That was a wonderful lunch. Thank you."

THE REST OF THE DAY had a dream-like quality about it. First a nap, then a leisurely walk with Oscar, and at the end of the day she sat down to another great meal with the family. She was in bed by nine o'clock.

She didn't know what woke her, and she lay still for a moment willing herself to go back to sleep before she realized that there was an unusual red glow flickering in the dark sky. The urgent banging on the back door and excited voices drew her out of bed and over to the open window.

"What's happened?" Maggie called down to the man on the back door step. She recognized him as Jim Robertson from the neighboring orchard.

But it was Bianca, who was dressed only in her night-gown, who called back up to her. "There's a fire! Jim's come to get Alonso."

"Where is it?"

"It's a little church on the far side of town—St. Martin's. The local fire brigade—which means all the able-bodied men in the town—are on their way. You may as well go back to bed. There's nothing we can do."

A minute later Maggie saw Alonso dash out of the house and get into Jim's truck, which was already turned around and ready to go. She looked at her watch. Two o'clock. She climbed back into bed, but it took her a long time to go back to sleep as she was now on edge, waiting to hear the men returning.

CHAPTER FOUR

Alonso didn't appear at the breakfast table.

"It was close to five when he got home," Bianca explained as she deftly flipped blueberry pancakes onto a serving platter. "He was totally exhausted. Help yourself from that pile on the table before the kids come downstairs and wolf them all."

"I never seem to have time to make pancakes," Maggie said as she placed three on her plate along with several strips of crisp bacon. Oscar was sitting as close to Maggie as he could, sniffing and giving a little whine as the tempting smell of the bacon wafted down to him. Surreptitiously she slipped him a morsel.

"It's a Sunday treat as it's our only free day from working and the kids don't have to go school."

"Did they put the fire out?" Maggie asked, reaching for the maple syrup.

Bianca nodded. "It's lucky the church walls were constructed of stone, but unfortunately the roof fell into the body of the church and did a fair amount of damage there before they had it under control."

"What a shame. Do they have any idea how it started?"

"Not yet. Alonso said the fire chief will be going through the building this morning." Suddenly the door to the kitchen was pushed open and Bellissa, Bianca's dark-haired daughter flew in, gave her mother a hug before turning to smile at Maggie. "I smelled pancakes," she said as she grabbed a plate and proceeded to pile it with food. "So were you two talking about the fire?"

"Yes," her mother said. "It is very sad."

"Well, I'm not surprised it burned down," Bellissa answered calmly. "It's pretty old. I wonder what old Schultzy will do now?"

"*Mister Schultz,*" Bianca remonstrated. "And he's not old. He's only in his mid-fifties."

"That's old!" Bellissa said.

Bianca shook her head in exasperation as she turned to Maggie. "Karl Schultz plays . . . I should say played . . . the organ at the church," she explained. "He's also a teacher at the high school in Penticton."

"Music?" Maggie asked.

"Among other subjects. The school's too small to have a full-time music teacher."

"What's going on?" Lorenzo, Bellisa's older brother, stood sleepily in the doorway, his black, curly hair uncombed. "Did I imagine it or did papa go out in the night?"

"St. Martin's burned to the ground," Bellisa told him dramatically. "How about we go have a look?"

"It didn't burn to the ground," Bianca corrected her, "and don't you two get in the way," she added. "The fire chief will have enough to do without dealing with a lot of gawkers."

"Oh mama, stop worrying." Bellisa turned to Maggie. "You want to come with us?"

Maggie shook her head. "I need a long walk after a breakfast like this. You can tell me all about it when I come back." She turned to Bianca who was still flipping pancakes and putting them in the warming oven. "I'll skip lunch."

"No need for that. I'll make a bag lunch for you to take with you."

Maggie patted her stomach. "No thanks, Bianca. I'll be fine."

IT WAS A PERFECT DAY for a walk down to the lake. Oscar, tail waving, trotted beside her, only stopping now and then to sniff where other dogs had gone before. When they reached the beach, Maggie removed her sandals and, walking barefoot on the fine sand, thought longingly of Nat and wished he was there with her.

"Hey there!"

Maggie, jolted out of her daydreaming, looked up to see a short woman bearing down on her. She was probably around the same age as herself, and she was hanging onto the leashes of two bull terriers.

"What kind of dog is he?" the woman demanded, nodding toward Oscar.

And Oscar, being the friendly animal he was, pulled Maggie over to inspect the new arrivals who wore bows pinned to their collars, one pink and the other blue. But the dog wearing the blue ribbon bared its teeth and gave a menacing growl.

Oscar knew that retreat was the better part of valour and quickly sidestepped so that it was Maggie who got the full impact of the lunging dog. The next thing she knew she was sitting on her rear end on the sand and Oscar had taken off along the beach, his leash flying in the wind, the two bull terriers hot on his heels.

"Help! Stop! Stop!" the owner of the terriers screeched. But the dogs, seeing their prey escaping along the shoreline, charged on, dragging the screaming woman behind them.

A pissed-off Maggie got to her feet as the quartet grew fainter in the distance. Then, imagining Oscar being mauled to pieces, she gathered up her sandals and handbag and charged after them.

She met them coming back a short time later. Oscar's leash was in the hands of a bald-headed man dressed in khaki shorts, blue short-sleeved shirt and leather sandals. The owner of the terriers was gazing up into the man's eyes adoringly as she talked to him, both her hands waving in the air for emphasis. Her two dogs, now panting and exhausted, walked dejectedly behind her.

"Oh, there you are," she greeted Maggie. "I was so lucky to run into dear Major Stroud who immediately took command. I was just telling him how naughty my puppies were to go chasing after your . . . your . . . what kind of dog did you say he was?"

"Oscar's a mutt, only I don't let him know that." She turned to the major. "Thanks so much for catching him for me."

"My pleasure," he answered with a slight bow as he handed the leash to her. "Now I must run along. Good afternoon, Mrs. Wallingford."

"I can't thank you enough, major. We must do lunch sometime."

"Uh, yes," he replied—rather reluctantly, Maggie thought.

"Such a nice man," the terriers' owner said to Maggie after the major had left. "He's divorced, you know." She held out her hand. "I'm Deidre Wallingford. You just moved here?"

"No. We're here on vacation."

Deidre leaned down and caressed Oscar's long ears. "You said 'we' so I take it you're not alone."

"I was referring to Oscar and myself," Maggie said stiffly.

"Oh, please don't mind me," Deidre said. "My husband always tells me I talk too much and that I should mind my own business. Why don't we sit on that log over there and let the dogs get acquainted?"

And Maggie found herself following with Oscar cowering behind her.

"And what did you say your name was?" Deidre asked, settling her large rump onto the log. "Hope I don't get any splinters," she added. "Wouldn't that be a laugh?"

Maggie, who couldn't think of anything worse, looked carefully before sitting. She realized that Deidre was waiting for an answer and guessed it wasn't about splinters. "I'm Maggie Spencer." The bull terriers, now off their leashes, were happily chasing a flock of unlucky gulls that had settled near them.

"So where are you staying?"

"The Rinaldis' guest house."

"Oh, that *Italian family*," Deirdre sniffed.

"They are wonderful hosts," Maggie said firmly.

Deidre grunted and continued. "Did you hear about the church being torched last night?"

"Yes. Mr. Rinaldi was called out to help."

"I heard that German organist Schultz has been taken in for questioning—you'd think the government would think twice about letting these foreigners into the country, especially the Germans and Italians. We could all be murdered in our beds," she added with relish.

Maggie's first impulse was to get up and leave the woman, but her curiosity got the better of her. "Why was he arrested?"

"Someone saw him running away from the church just after it burst into flames."

"Who could possibly have seen him in the middle of the night?"

The woman shrugged. "Everyone knows that he plays the organ in the church."

"But it was the middle of the night!" Maggie repeated. "How could anyone see him?"

"I'm only repeating what I've heard," Deidre Wallingford replied huffily before abruptly changing the subject. "So what made you pick Naramata for a vacation?"

"Just passing through," Maggie answered, standing up. "Come along, Oscar."

"What's your hurry?"

"Bianca's expecting me for lunch," she lied as she bent and fastened the dog's leash. "Nice to have met you, Mrs. Wallingford. Come along, Oscar."

Cavendish's Curios, the village's souvenir and ice cream shop, was busy and Maggie had to wait quite a while to pay for the postcards she picked out. Of course, the general conversation in the shop was the fire and Karl Schultz having been taken in for questioning.

"That's a German for you," an elderly man stated. "I was in the Great War, you know, and I . . ."

"None of us is safe," a woman interrupted with relish.

"Oh, for God's sake," buxom Mrs. Cavendish said, pausing in the act of making change for a customer. "Karl has lived here for years and," she added, "he's a real gentleman. Just the postcards?" she asked, turning to Maggie. "They're ten cents each. If you need stamps, you'll have to come back tomorrow because it's Sunday and the post office is closed."

The talk came to an abrupt stop while Maggie paid for her purchases, and all eyes were upon her as she pushed her way past the customers and out the shop door. Once outside, she took a lung full of fresh air and then turned in the direction of the Rinaldis' apple orchard. "What nasty people," she muttered. Oscar looked up at her enquiringly.

CHAPTER FIVE

There were at least ten people in the Rinaldi kitchen, and they, like those in the village shop, were all talking at once. Maggie only recognized the Rinaldis' neighbours, Jim and Marjorie Robertson, and sensing there was a meeting of some kind in process, she tried to by-pass the kitchen and slip upstairs to her room.

"Wait, Maggie!" Bianca called after her. "You can help us? Si?"

"Me? How?"

"You are a detective?"

Maggie hesitated. "Not a police detective. I assist my partner in an investigating agency. And why do you want a detective?"

Marjorie Robertson cut in, "We just need some advice."

"Advice?"

"It's to do with Karl. He's been arrested."

"And we have to help him," Bianca said.

"There's not much you can do to help him if the police have evidence that he started that fire," Maggie said firmly.

"But it's not just the fire," Jim Robertson answered. The room went quiet. "You see, the police and the fire chief had to wait until this morning before they could get into the building and. . . and they found the body of a young man, and it looks as if he was murdered. They've taken Karl in for questioning."

"Murdered?" Maggie asked. "How do they know he was murdered?"

"Our volunteer fire chief told us. He was the one that found him. He said the victim had 'sustained a terrible injury to his head.' Those are his words."

"Karl phoned Jim from the main police station in Penticton," Bianca cut in. "He was in quite a state and insisted that he had returned home way before the fire began."

"And. . . ? Maggie asked.

"The police don't believe him because someone said they'd seen him running away from the church just before the place went up in smoke."

"Isn't there someone who can verify his whereabouts?"

"He lives alone, unfortunately," Jim explained. "I'm on my way to Penticton to see if I can get in there to talk to him."

Bianca turned to Maggie. "You go with Jim and talk to Karl. He is such a good man. He wouldn't hurt anybody."

"But I don't know him, and I certainly can't interfere in a police investigation," Maggie explained. But her protests fell on deaf ears as Bianca took Oscar's leash from her hands and then gently pushed her toward the door. Maggie was still protesting as Jim helped her up into his ancient truck, and then she found talk was impossible over the noisy engine and the rattles and bangs from the rusty vehicle.

Jim Robertson parked across the road from the police station and, after helping Maggie down, took her by the arm and propelled her through the door and up to the desk.

"We want to talk to Karl Schultz."

"Are you a relative?"

"No. I'm Jim Robertson, his friend and neighbour."

"Has Mr. Schultz been charged?" Maggie asked the man behind the desk.

The officer looked Maggie up and down. "Are you a lawyer?"

"No. Does he need one?"

"You better talk to Sergeant Allen. Take a seat."

After what seemed an eternity, the inner door opened. A tall officer, who Maggie took to be Sergeant Allen, walked over to where they were sitting. "I understand you are friends of Mr. Schultz?"

Jim nodded. "We would like to talk to him."

The officer looked them over coldly. "We are pre-pared to release him on the understanding that he stays in Naramata until we have finalized our investigation. Are you willing to be responsible for his release, Mr. Robert-son?"

"Of course we will. Where do we sign?"

"We need verification that you are residents of Nara-mata. Constable Denver will get you both to sign a release form."

"I'm not a resident," Maggie announced.

Sergeant Allen turned to her. "You're not Mrs. Robertson?"

"No. I'm staying with Mr. and Mrs. Renaldi."

The sergeant was perplexed. "But you are a friend of Karl Schultz?"

Maggie shook her head and reluctantly opened her purse and produced one of her agency cards. "I'm on vacation here. Karl's neighbours thought perhaps I could help."

Allen took the card, scanned it and then glared at her with his piercing blue eyes. "I do hope you are not even thinking of interfering in police matters, Miss. . .uh. . .Miss Spencer."

"Actually it's Mrs. And I wouldn't dream of interfering. I am, as I said, here on a well-earned vacation."

Allen looked down at the card once more before slipping it into his breast pocket. "Just see that's all you do."

A good half hour later the inner door opened once more and a man of medium height, probably in his late fifties and somewhat overweight, peered myopically through thick pebble glasses as he stumbled toward them. His tired face lit up on seeing his friend Jim. "How good of you to come! I apologise for my appearance, but I didn't sleep very well last night."

"Let's get you home," Jim replied, taking the man by the arm. "This is Maggie Spencer."

"Maggie Spencer?" Karl looked puzzled but allowed himself to be pushed through the door and out into the late afternoon sunshine and—for the time being—freedom.

"Oh, my cane. . ." He turned to walk back into the station. "I left it in that cell where they kept me."

"I'll get it for you," Maggie said. "You two get over to the truck." She returned a short time later carrying his silver-knobbed, ebony walking stick.

"Thank you," Karl said, taking it from her. "It was my father's and I would hate to lose it."

The ride back to Naramata was even more uncomfortable than the trip into town. Maggie was now wedged in the middle of the vinyl-covered bench seat, and every bump or turn of the unpaved road slid her against one man or the other, while they shouted over her head, trying to talk over the noisy engine.

Jim had stopped at the telephone box opposite the police station to phone home, and the neighbours were waiting at the B&B to welcome Karl back. He was ushered into the Renaldi kitchen where a table was laden down with food—Bianca had been busy. Maggie could see that Karl was exhausted, but he graciously sat down at the head of the table and let Bianca fill a glass with wine for him.

Accepting the glass, he stared around the table, "You must believe me when I tell you I did not do this terrible thing."

"Si, si, we know." Alonso stood behind him and patted his shoulder. "Eat up and then you have a good sleep."

"Yes, I must get home."

"No," Bianca said firmly, "you're staying with us tonight."

"But. . ."

Maggie could see the man was too exhausted to argue. "Have the police any idea who the dead man was?" she asked.

"I don't think so," Karl said. "But they seem to think that I know." His voice broke and unbidden tears slipped down his face. "I kept telling them I left the church before ten o'clock, but they wouldn't listen."

"We will leave it all until tomorrow. For now, just eat up." Bianca was of the old school that firmly believed a glass of good wine and some home cooking could resolve all problems.

Maggie, watching Karl pushing the food around the plate and only taking small sips of the wine, took pity on him. "Come on," she said, getting to her feet and taking him by the arm. "A good sleep will do wonders for you. Bianca, where is Karl to sleep?"

"Come with me, Karl," Bianca said and escorted him up the stairs.

Maggie turned to Jim Robertson. "Was the victim burned beyond recognition?"

"I don't think so," he answered slowly. "After all, the fire chief could see that it was a young man with a terrible head injury—so he couldn't have been that badly burned."

"But I understood the fire completely gutted the church. . . "

"No, no," Alonso said. "We put the fire out quick. Lots of damage to the walls inside, and part of the roof she fall down, so the chief he say no one was to go inside until it all cool down."

"It seems that a falling roof beam toppled the pulpit," Jim Robertson explained, "and when the chief and a couple of firemen lifted it up, they found the dead man wedged underneath. I guess it shielded the body from being completely burned."

"If he was crushed by the pulpit," Maggie said slowly, "it means he was not necessarily murdered. He may have been sleeping in the church and been asphyxiated when the fire started. Then the pulpit fell on him. . ."

Jim shook his head. "There's no way the pulpit falling on him could have caused the kind of injuries the chief said he had. Anyway, it was the iron bar lying beside the pulpit that caught the chief's attention. That's when he saw the young man's feet sticking out."

"How awful," Bianca said.

Jim nodded. "It's going to be a long time before Sam gets over it." He turned to Maggie. "Sam Lightfoot's our fire chief," he explained.

"And poor Karl is being blamed for the death," Marjorie Robertson said as she helped herself from the bowl of pasta.

There was silence again as everyone contemplated this fact, then Maggie asked, "Who was it claimed they saw Karl running away from the burning building?"

"Georgina Jennings."

"That old busybody," Marjorie exclaimed. "Why would the police believe something she said?"

"I'll take you over to see her in the morning," Bianca told Maggie. "Then you can ask her questions."

"I can't interfere in a police investigation," Maggie protested.

"You go with Bianca and get to the bottom of this terrible thing," Alonso said. He ladled out a huge bowl of pasta and reached across the table to place it in front of her. "Now you eat up."

Maggie looked at the earnest faces around the table and thought, *Oh, my God! How am I going to explain this to Nat?*

CHAPTER SIX

"I don't know how you do it, Maggie!" was Nat's first reaction. "Why couldn't you have a simple vacation like everyone else?"

"Well, I can't just up and leave, can I?"

She had left the supper table as soon as she could, pleading a headache that only a brisk walk would cure. Thankfully, the village's only public telephone booth, which stood outside the post office, was unoccupied, and Nat had answered right away as if he had been sitting there waiting for her call. It had taken quite a while to explain the situation to him because he kept interrupting. Finally, totally exasperated, she had yelled at him to "calm down and listen!" Then she explained how her hosts had insisted on her going to the Penticton police, that she was sure there was a perfectly good explanation, that somebody had identified Karl as the man running away from the church, and that as soon as things had settled down, she would be on her way. "So you can see that I can't just up and leave here."

"Yes, you bloody well can!" Nat exploded. "You can't run a murder investigation on your own! It's time for you to come home!"

"I'll be back when my vacation time is up. Which, let me remind you, won't be for another fourteen days." She slammed the receiver down hard. "Why can't he under-stand?" Then she felt a mite guilty as she knew how much he cared for her. But it wasn't her fault that murders seemed to pop up when and where she least expected them. *I'll call him tomorrow when I know more.* Leaving the telephone booth, she walked determinedly back to the Apple Orchard Guest House.

NAT REPLACED THE PHONE and leaned back in his easy chair. "What am I going to do with you, Maggie?" He sat staring at the phone, willing her to call him back but knowing she wouldn't. Reaching for the bottle of Scotch on the side table, he poured himself a hefty one and took an appreciative swig. "I'll call this place where she's stay-ing first thing in the morning."

But Nat hardly slept after Maggie's phone call. He tossed and turned and went round and round their conver-sation, becoming more and more agitated about how she wouldn't listen to reason. And in the light of morning he realized that it was no good calling her back. He knew that when she made up her mind on something, there usually wasn't anything he could do or say to make her change it.

He explained all this to George as soon as he arrived at the office. "I don't know how she gets involved in these situations, and it's always when I'm not there to make her see sense."

His friend laughed. "You should listen to yourself, pal. You're the one that's been encouraging her to think for herself, and when she does, you worry that you're not there to guide her. Your Maggie is one smart lady and, by the look of things, the friends she's made in Naramata think she is too. Otherwise they wouldn't have asked her to help."

"But she's not qualified to take on a murder investigation."

"I agree. So I think if she needs help, she'll call for it." He leaned back in his chair. "In fact, isn't that what she did by calling you last night?"

"I can't just pull up stakes and go rushing to the Okanagan. You know how busy we are here right now."

"That's why you've taken me on," George answered. "But Maggie will tell you when she needs your help. You can depend on that."

Nat sighed. "I guess you're right. I just can't help worrying about her and the scrapes she gets herself into."

George grinned. "That's called love, old pal."

LIKE NAT, MAGGIE ALSO had a problem sleeping. The phone call to Nat still rankled, but mostly she was kept awake by her need to find out more about the fire and the murder of the unknown man. *I'll talk to Karl first thing in the morning and then call on the woman who insisted she saw him running away from the fire.* With that settled in her mind, she tried to compose herself for sleep, but it was well after three before she finally dropped off.

She awoke to brilliant sunshine flooding the room, and a glance at the alarm clock on the bedside table told her it was after nine and she had overslept. The house was eerily quiet. Of course, she thought, Bianca and Alonso would be working in the orchard, and Bellisa and her brother were most probably in school, but perhaps Karl would still be around and she could ask him a few questions. She dressed quickly and dashed down to the kitchen. A place had been set for her at the scrubbed pine table with a note to help herself to whatever she wanted for breakfast—but there was no sign of Karl Schultz.

"We were up so early and I didn't like to wake you," Bianca explained when Maggie and Oscar finally tracked her down on the far side of the orchard. "The weather forecast is for thunderstorms and that could mean hail," she continued, "so we must get as many of the Golden Delicious picked as we can. Some of our neighbours have come to help, too."

Maggie surveyed the darkening clouds edging over the mountains to the west. "I'll help." Quickly donning a spare picking bag, she asked, "Where do you want me to start?"

"You okay with ladders?" Bianca asked as she expertly threw the third leg of a fourteen-foot-tall, wide-angled ladder toward the trunk of the next apple tree in the row.

Maggie nodded, hoping she was.

"We sure can do with every bit of help," Bianca said, watching Maggie's slow progress up the ladder. "But please be careful. We don't want to send you back to Vancouver with a broken arm or something."

Oscar, also watching Maggie as she climbed, gave a big sigh, curled himself into a ball and settled at the foot of the tree. His walk would have to wait. While they picked, Bianca explained that, although it was late in the year for hail, it had happened this late the previous year and the damage to the apples had cut their profits considerably.

They worked all morning and once Maggie had got into the rhythm of picking and unloading her bag, she found that she was thoroughly enjoying the physical labour. She was down from the ladder and in the process of picking from the lower branches of her tree when the first fat rain drops started to fall.

"Maggie, get up to the house before you get soaked," Bianca called. "The other pickers will finish up here. You'll find a pot of soup in the fridge. Could you put it on to heat, please? I've invited everybody to come up to the house for lunch. . ."

Maggie was happy to head for the house, and once there she rubbed Oscar down, then quickly peeled off her grubby, wet clothes and let the soothing water of a hot shower ease her aching body. But as soon as she turned off the water, she heard the dreaded, apple-damaging hail pounding on the roof. Dressed once again, she headed down to the kitchen to start preparations for lunch. She was heating the pot of minestrone soup she'd found in the fridge when Bianca burst through the outer door.

"Oh, Maggie, you are a dear. I'll just change and be down to help." True to her word, Bianca soon reappeared in the kitchen and began setting places on the long pine table. Piles of home-made bread, Italian sausage, cheeses, tomatoes and grapes followed. "Okay, now you sit," she commanded Maggie. "I will serve the soup and you help yourself because once Alonso and the others arrive they will clear the table in no time flat."

"How much damage did the hail do?" Maggie asked.

"We won't know until we get our returns from the packing house. But we won't think about that now. Just you eat up."

Maggie grabbed a large piece of bread and happily dug her spoon into the thick broth. "Where do you get these delicious grapes?" she asked, pointing at the pile on the table. "You always seem to have a ready supply of them."

"Oh, that's one of Alonso's experiments. A few years ago he realized that the soil and climate here are almost the same as in our valley in Italy, so he got his father to ship him some cuttings."

"And they took?" Maggie asked.

Bianca nodded. "This is the best year so far. He's seriously thinking of putting a larger part of the orchard into grapes. Of course, most of the apple growers around here are quite sure he's mad."

"I can't see why," Maggie said, piling ham, cheese, tomatoes and some of the grapes onto her plate, "it's a wonderful idea. I can see you producing your own wine in a few years."

"That's Alonso's ambition. Oh, here come the pickers. I hope I have enough soup for everyone."

Maggie ate her lunch hurriedly and left the table. She and Oscar had been back in their room for nearly an hour when she suddenly remembered that Bianca was going to take her to see the witness who swore she'd seen Karl running away. "I wonder if she's still in the kitchen," she said to Oscar. "Bianca," she called as she ran down the stairs, "you said you would take me to talk to Georgina Jennings."

"Oh, Maggie, I'm so sorry," Bianca said as she struggled into her raincoat. "I completely forgot, and I don't have time to take you now. We have to load the last of the peaches on the truck to take to that roadside stand I told you about." She glanced at the old-fashioned kitchen clock on the wall. "It's going to take a couple of hours."

"Don't worry. Just give me the address and tell me how to get there. After all, Naramata isn't such a big a town that I can get lost."

"FAMOUS LAST WORDS," Maggie muttered an hour later as she shielded Bianca's sketchy instructions from the rain in order to re-read them. "It's got to be round here somewhere." Oscar just wagged his tail. He didn't mind being lost.

The houses were built fairly close to the road, and she was about to admit defeat and knock on any door to ask for directions to Church Road, when the acrid smell of burned wood tickled her nostrils. That was when she re-called Bianca telling her that Georgina Jennings lived just a few houses from the church. So she must be close. The smell led her one street over, and there halfway down it was the charred remains of the church, and number 145 was across the street and just three houses down.

Bedraggled marigolds lined the path that led up to a wooden door that sported a highly polished brass horse's head knocker. The window to the left of the door had a notice declaring in large print that hawkers, beggars or other such persons were not welcome, and Maggie wondered if that included private investigators. The window to the right of the door had a sign saying there was a room for rent. She lifted the knocker.

The door immediately opened to reveal a tall woman, probably in her late sixties, dressed in a black skirt, white blouse and black cardigan, her grey-streaked hair pulled back into a neat bun. She looked Maggie up and down and then turned her gaze disapprovingly on Oscar, who was doing his best to hide behind Maggie.

"I don't take dogs," she said.

"It's about the fire," Maggie said hastily before the woman could close the door. "Just a few questions."

"You one of those reporters?"

"No. I'm an investigator. Look, if you'll let me come in, I'll explain."

"I told the police what I saw." The woman began edging the door closed again.

"I know. But perhaps you wouldn't mind explaining something to me." Maggie held out one of her cards. "It will only take a few minutes." She hated having to wheedle.

"That animal has to stay outside."

"Okay. Sit, Oscar." With a woebegone look at Maggie, he complied, and she tied the end of his leash to the porch railings and followed Georgina Jennings into a narrow front hallway and from there into a living room that overlooked the street. Starched lace curtains covered the bay window and shielded the inevitable rubber plant. Antimacassars were arrayed on a pristine three-piece velour suite. Two spindly end tables were decorated with white lace doilies. On one was a sepia photo of a man in military garb and on the other was a photo of a stern elderly couple. *Must be her parents. They have the same sour look.* She was not invited to sit.

"So what do you want to know?"

"I understand you were the one that reported seeing Karl Schultz running away from the burning church?"

"Yes. Saw him as plain as day. I woke up when I heard a noise and then I saw him running away before the fire was discovered. He set that fire and then ran away. I told the police all that."

"But how were you so sure it was him? It was what . . . nearly two o'clock in the morning? Wasn't it dark at that hour?"

Georgina Jennings drew in a deep breath. "No, it was earlier than that. As I just told you, he ran away *before* the fire was discovered."

"So, was that about one o'clock?"

"Probably. . .yes, around one o'clock. But the real clincher was that *stupid* cape he wears." She sniffed. "He goes swanning around the town in it as if he is above everyone else. He's a filthy German!" she spat. "That's all he is, a filthy German."

Maggie, realizing she'd better change her tactics, walked over to the window, carefully parted the curtains and looked out. "I didn't realize how close you are to the church."

"That's how I knew it was that German. Saw him as plain as day," she repeated.

"Actually he comes from Strasburg, Saskatchewan, and," Maggie said quietly, "he is a third generation Canadian citizen." She had learned these facts from Bianca and she couldn't resist informing this woman.

"As I was saying," Georgina Jennings said, totally ignoring Maggie's explanation, "it was that German that I saw running away from the fire like a coward."

"So it was a noise that woke you?"

The woman gave Maggie a sharp look. "Couldn't go back to sleep after that. And a good thing, too. It was me that phoned that so-called fire brigade, and I can tell you they took their time getting here."

"So your bedroom is on the other side of this hallway," Maggie said pointing.

"If it's any business of yours, my bedroom's upstairs."

"Overlooking the street?" Maggie persisted.

"No. I keep the front bedroom for paying guests."

"So your bedroom is at the back of the house? So it must've been a *very* loud noise to have disturbed your sleep? Perhaps it was made by one of your paying guests?"

"I don't have any boarders at present." She glared at Maggie. "You sure you're not from one of those papers?" She marched out of the room and opened the front door. "I suggest you talk to the police and not come calling honest people liars."

It was quite plain the interview was over. Outside, Oscar was very pleased to see Maggie and jumped up and down as if she had been away hours instead of minutes. She turned back to say goodbye, but the door was already firmly shut and the lace curtains in the bay window hid the sitting room from sight.

Crossing over the road, Maggie walked toward the little church and stood sadly considering it.

"It's quite a mess, isn't it?"

Startled, Maggie looked up to see a man wearing a buttoned-up black raincoat and a dripping tweed hat.

"Sorry, I didn't mean to frighten you." He thrust out a hand. "Anthony Bicknell. I'm the rector here. Haven't seen you around so I guess you're visiting."

Maggie nodded. "I'm Maggie Spencer. I'm so sorry this has happened." She hesitated for a moment. "I imagine you're very upset that your organist is being blamed for the fire."

"It's absolutely ridiculous," Bicknell exploded. "How could anyone suspect such a gentle person as Karl Schultz of arson? I told that RCMP officer that I had talked with Karl on the phone at 7:30—he was here at the church practising—and we talked on the phone to decide on the music for Sunday evening's service." When Maggie looked confused, he said, "Oh, I'm not here on Saturdays, you see. I'm in charge of St. Mary's in Kelowna as well as St. Martin's and I don't come to Naramata until Sunday afternoon." When she nodded, he continued, "I phoned back to the church around 9:30 or so to change one of the hymns, but he must have already gone home, and apparently the fire didn't start until sometime in the wee hours of the morning." He stopped. "Oh, I'm so sorry—I'm sure you're not interested in all this."

"As a matter of fact, I am." Maggie opened her bag and once again produced one of her business cards. "Friends of Karl have asked me to look into the accusations. They, like you, don't believe that he would set fire to the church. They said that he loved playing the organ too much to destroy it."

"That's wonderful. If there's anything I can do. . ." His voice trailed off.

"Thanks. I'm off to see Karl now, but I might take you up on your offer."

So that explains why the rector didn't call the fire department, Maggie thought as she walked away. He wasn't here on Saturday night. He was in Kelowna.

The rain had stopped by the time she reached the main street and located Karl Schultz's house on a nearby side street. It was a clapboard, two-storied building much like all the others lining the street with the same very neat, small fenced-in garden in front. But as she walked up the concrete path to the wooden front door and peered through the living room window beside it and saw a baby grand piano, she was pretty sure she had come to the right house.

It was a few minutes before Karl, leaning heavily on his cane, cautiously opened the door. "Oh, it's you, Mrs. Spencer." Glancing anxiously up and down the street, he continued, "Do come in, and you'd better bring your companion with you," he added, looking down at the bedraggled dog. He bent to rub Oscar's ears. "What kind of dog is he?"

"A bit of a mixture, as you can see," Maggie said, laughing. "But as you say, a great companion."

He led them through to the kitchen where she accepted the towel he offered to rub Oscar down, and when she was finished, she sat in the chair he indicated.

"What a lovely bright room," she said. A watery sun was doing its best to filter through the large window to light up the gleaming pots and pans that hung over the stove.

He handed her a cup of coffee and she took an appreciative sip. "And I sure needed this. Would you mind answering a few questions for me?"

"But, Mrs. Spencer, I can't tell you much except that I didn't set that fire."

"Let's go over that day anyway." She flipped her notebook open and poised her pen. "Start from when you got up."

Karl sighed. "Well, if you think it will help." He gazed into the distance before he spoke. "I woke up early as usual only to remember that it was Saturday so I didn't have to go to Penticton to teach. I love teaching," he assured her, "but I really look forward to my weekends."

"Me, too," Maggie answered. "Saturday was September 15th, wasn't it? I seem to have lost track of time since I came here."

"Yes, it was the 15th. I had a leisurely breakfast and then drove to Penticton to buy my groceries for the week."

"Did you speak to anyone in Penticton?"

"Just the girl in the grocery store," he answered. "I stopped at a roadside stall to buy homemade bread and a jar of honey. I got home around eleven." He stopped, looking pensive.

"And then. . .?"

"After lunch I gave an hour's music lesson to Brian Wallingford." Karl gave a wry smile. "Nice boy, but his mother is a bit. . ." he paused, searching for the right word, ". . . a bit difficult."

Maggie smiled. "I've met the lady in question."

"Ah! She has rather high expectations of her ten-year-old son, and he. . .well, he is not exactly musically inclined. After he left, I did some tidying up in the garden, read the newspapers I'd bought that morning and then cooked myself some supper."

"And after supper. . .?" Maggie prompted.

"I walked over to St. Martin's to go over the music for the next day. I'm not Anglican, but I've been helping the rector out by playing the organ for Sunday evening services. It's really quite a nice instrument for such a small church. . ." Then his face fell. "I should have said '*was* a nice instrument,' shouldn't I? It was probably burned along with the church."

"How long did you practise?"

"I lose track of time when I'm playing, but probably a couple of hours or so." He gave Maggie a sad smile. "I'm quite the absent-minded professor, you know."

"Was it fully dark when you left the church?"

"No, no. It wasn't completely dark yet, but it was a beautiful evening, and there was a full moon just coming up. Oh yes, and I remember that when I reached home, I turned on the radio and the ten o'clock news had already started. So it must have been getting very close to ten when I left the church."

Damn! Maggie thought. *A full moon! That would have helped Georgina Jennings to identify the arsonist.* Then another thought occurred to her. "Reverend Bicknell says he called you again at 9:30 and you didn't answer so he thought you had already gone home."

Karl Schultz looked away guiltily. "No, I was still there, and I did hear the phone ringing in the vestry. You see, I knew who it would be. Tony has this habit of calling back to change the hymns at the last moment, and . . ."

"And you didn't want to change them because you'd already practised the first list of hymns."

He nodded.

"Did you go out again that night?"

"You mean to torch the church?" he answered ruefully. "No. I listened to the radio news and went to bed."

"Do you own a black cape?"

"Yes, I do. Why do you ask?"

"When was the last time you wore it?"

"Not for a long time. It's rather thick and the weather's been so warm, though I could have done with it on Saturday night because it was a bit nippy on my way home."

"Do you realize that's how Mrs. Jennings identified you that night? She said she saw you running away from the church, and you were wearing your cape."

"That's ridiculous!" Then he smiled and added, "Besides, my running days are long over."

"Did you by any chance leave your cape in the church?"

"No, no." And he got up and left the room. A few minutes later he returned carrying a voluminous black cape over his arm. "It's quite heavy so I only wear it when the weather gets cold."

"So now the big question is," Maggie said, "who was the person Georgina Jennings saw running away from the fire wearing a cape? And was that person the arsonist and the murderer?" She rose from the table and bent to attach Oscar's leash. When she straightened up, she asked, "How do you put up with bigoted people like Mrs. Jennings?"

"Ah yes. . . But you see, most of the children I teach are not bigoted even if their parents are," he said.

"Mr. Schultz," Maggie said abruptly, moving to get a better look out of the kitchen window. "I think there's someone in your back yard."

At that moment there was a loud banging on the back door.

"Who can that be?" Karl asked worriedly as he opened the door and then stepped back in surprise. Sergeant Allen stood there with his hand raised ready to bang again.

"Do you own a black cape?"

"Again?" Karl exclaimed. "Yes, I do. Here it is." He thrust it at the sergeant. "So what's all this about my cape?"

Allen replied, "We have received new information that the person seen running from the church on the night of the fire was wearing a black cape."

"Georgina Jennings," Maggie said disgustedly.

The sergeant inclined his head toward Maggie. "That's none of your business, and I have already told you to stay out of this case!" He turned his back and started to walk away, the cape under his arm.

"Sergeant, can you tell me where the fire actually started?" she called after him.

"That's classified information, Mrs. Spencer." He continued to walk away.

LATER, WHEN MAGGIE WAS having supper with the Rinaldi family, she put the same question to Alonso.

He paused with his fork in mid-air. "It was cigarette butt in waste basket."

"Where?" Maggie asked.

"The pastor's office."

"But a fire in a waste basket wouldn't be enough to burn the church down!"

Alonso waved a hand at the kitchen curtains. "You see, it burn curtains." And he stood up to demonstrate flames mounting the curtains and climbing up to the ceiling. "We get there and roof she is already coming down!"

Maggie nodded. "Georgina Jennings said she was awakened by a loud noise."

"That must have been when the rafters fell," Bianca said.

And Lorenzo added, "It made enough noise to wake the dead."

"But she told me she sleeps in a back room of her house," Maggie said. "Would she have heard the rafters falling from there?"

Bianca shook her head. "I don't know. . ."

"And anyway," Maggie continued, "she said it was *after* she was wakened by a loud noise that she saw someone running away, and that was nearly an hour *before* the fire was discovered. There's something not right here."

CHAPTER SEVEN

George Sawasky looked up as Nat appeared in the office doorway.

"We've got a new client coming in this morning," Nat said. "It's a woman by the name of Fiona Phelps. Apparently her eighteen-year-old brother disappeared about two weeks ago."

George shook his head. "If I had a nickel for every teen-aged boy whose family reported him missing, only to have him turn up a few days later a little worn but wiser, I'd be a rich man! This kid will probably turn up in his own good time."

"That was my first reaction, but she absolutely won't agree. She said that Gordon—that's the boy's name—has just graduated top of his class from Lord Byng, he's happy at home and looking forward to his first year at UBC. He plans to become a doctor. . ."

"What about his parents?"

"She said she'd explain that situation when she gets here. How about joining me in my office and we can deal with this together?"

George stood, collected his cup of coffee and notebook and followed Nat to his office. Ten minutes later Henny announced their client, and both men stood up as a tall, red-haired woman, her green eyes enhanced by stylish glasses, walked in and extended a gloved hand over the desk to Nat. She seemed a lot older that he had expected—probably in her late thirties.

"Fiona Phelps," she said.

"And this is my associate, George Sawasky. Please have a seat."

She was dressed in a well-cut gabardine suit, and she adjusted her skirt carefully before sitting. "I was hoping to meet with Mrs. Spencer. She was very well recommended to me."

"At the moment she's on a well-earned vacation. But I'm sure we can help you. You said on the phone that your brother has disappeared. Have you heard from him since then?"

"No, and I'm at my wit's end—there's my parents, you see."

"They don't know about Gordon's disappearance?" George hazarded.

She shook her head. "I haven't told them. They are elderly and neither of them is exactly in good health." She paused for a moment. "Gordon was what you might call a late-in-life baby, and I was the one who really brought him up."

"So when was the last time you saw your brother?"

"August 31st. He went to the Okanagan for the Labour Day weekend with one of his friends from high school—Adam Herrmann. I don't know the boy, but his parents have a summer place there. . . " She gave a wan smile. "In Summerland."

"So what do the Herrmann boy's parents do for a living?" Nat asked.

"Some kind of textile business . . .tents, I think."

"And August 31st was definitely the last time you heard from your brother?" George asked.

"Yes. He was supposed to be back by September 4th to prepare for university. You know, to buy books and clothes and that kind of thing. . ."

"I guess you called the Herrmann boy's parents?"

She nodded. "Of course, but I got no answer. And that was two weeks ago and I have been phoning and phoning ever since."

"Did the boys go to the Okanagan by car?" George asked.

"Yes. I gave Gordon a car when he graduated from high school. He's a very competent driver."

"And the Herrmann boy—was he going to travel back to the coast with Gordon?" George asked.

"Yes," she said.

"And you've called the police?"

She nodded. "Several times. They gave me the old platitude that boys-will-be-boys and he'll turn up. They insist they've checked for accidents and hospitals and there's nothing to indicate foul play."

"Can you give me the Herrmanns' address?" Nat asked, pen poised over his pad.

"I have it here somewhere." She rummaged deep in her brown leather handbag then said, almost as if she was surprised, "Oh, here's a photograph of Gordon." She handed it across the desk and delved back into the bag, this time producing a sheet of paper. "Here we are. You see that I have written down both their Summerland and Vancouver addresses." She rose from her chair. "And of course, you have my address."

"Thanks," Nat said, taking the list. "Your parents have to be told, you know."

"Yes. But I'd like to wait until we have something concrete to tell them."

"What kind of car does your brother drive?" George asked.

"It's a blue 1957 Impala."

"I don't suppose you know the licence plate number?"

"Actually I do. It's 103-462."

"I think that's all we need for the moment," Nat said, standing up. "If you wouldn't mind stopping at Henny's desk on the way out, she'll explain our terms and have you fill out the customary form."

"So you will take this on?"

"Yes. I'll keep you informed all the way."

"Nice looking boy," Nat remarked after Fiona had left. He examined the photo for a few more minutes before handing it over to George.

The colour photograph showed a red-haired young man at the wheel of a motor launch. He was dressed in blue swimming trunks and he had partly turned to laugh at the person holding the camera.

"Very nice," George said dryly. "You can see the re-semblance to his sister, especially the hair colour. Of course, her hair could be dyed," he added. "So what do you want me to do?"

"The usual. Contact the police and the hospitals here and in the Okanagan. Check with the Herrmanns—perhaps they're back by now." He was quiet for a few moments. "Come to think of it, Maggie isn't all that far from Summerland—I might as well ask her to check that address out."

"But she's on vacation," George protested.

Nat grinned. "She'd kill me if she found out I hadn't included her."

"AND YOU WANT ME to drive to Summerland to check this out?" Maggie asked after Nat had told her of their inability to locate Gordon Phelps' friend Adam Herrmann or Adam's parents. "Actually, Nat, although I can see Summerland across the lake from here, it'll take at least half an hour for me to get there by road."

"Yes, I know I've got a lot of cheek asking this when you're on holiday. . ."

She interrupted him. "You've tried their Vancouver address?"

"Yes, and George has called Herrmann Brothers Tent and Awning. It's off Clark Drive on the east side of the city. It's co-owned by Peter Herrmann—he's Adam's father—and Peter's brother, Wilhelm."

"Did George speak to either of them?" Maggie asked.

"He got Wilhelm on the phone, and he said Peter is having family problems and had extended his vacation for at least another couple of weeks."

"Did he say where he was?"

"No. He told George that Peter and his wife were 'travelling'."

"I wonder why he's being so cagey . . ."

"And where are they?" Nat insisted. "It's seems very strange that they disappeared at the same time that Gordon Phelps went missing."

Maggie was quiet for a moment. "Have you got a description of this young man? You know—age, hair colour, type of car he was driving?"

Nat breathed an inward sigh of relief as he answered her. "So you will look into it? His sister gave us a photograph and description. He's eighteen, about 5'11", slim build, red hair, green eyes. He's driving a 1957 blue Impala, licence 103-462."

"Okay. I'll call into the Penticton police station first thing tomorrow and then drive on to Summerland. What's the Herrmanns' address there?"

CHAPTER EIGHT

"**B**usy?" George asked as he put his head around the door to Nat's office.

"What's up?"

"I've had no luck in getting in touch with the Herrmanns. I've tried the Summerland number a dozen times, and last night I dropped by the place they have on West 12th again. Nobody answered the door, and the neighbours I talked to said that they hadn't seen them for weeks. The woman said she thought they were in the Okanagan."

"Has the boy Adam returned?"

"That's odd, too. I phoned Fiona Phelps to see if Adam was planning to take the same courses as her brother, and she said that as far as she knew he wasn't going to university. He was going straight into his father's tent and awning business, so the uncle should know where he is, don't you think?"

"Right," Nat said. "We're going to visit the uncle."

THE NEXT MORNING MAGGIE'S little red car hummed along the narrow road that led into Penticton with a very happy Oscar sitting regally in the passenger seat. All was well in his doggy world. The rain had stopped, the sky was azure blue, and the sun was pleasantly warm for a mid-September day.

The duty officer at the police station frowned as Maggie walked in.

"Is Sergeant Allen available?" she asked.

"If you'll give me your name and take a seat over there, I'll see."

Maggie sat on one of the hard wooden chairs, and as she prepared for a long wait in the dusty, sterile room, she thought about her conversation with Nat the night before. *There has to be a logical explanation for the whole Herrmann family to disappear. Though, of course, they may have just taken themselves off on a family holiday somewhere, and there may be no connection to Gordon Phelps' disappearance at all.*

"Mrs. Spencer, what can I do for you?"

Maggie was so engrossed in her speculations that she gave a visible jump.

"Sorry, didn't mean to startle you," Sergeant Allen said.

"I just wanted to ask a couple of questions."

"You'd better come through to my office," he said, leading the way behind the duty officer's desk. "You understand I can't discuss an ongoing investigation."

"Yes. I understand, but my partner, Nat Southby, is looking into a teenager's disappearance," Maggie began before she even sat down in the chair opposite him. "The boy was staying with a friend in Summerland and apparently left to drive home the day after Labour Day, but he never arrived."

"Your partner has contacted the Summerland detachment?"

Maggie nodded. "And the hospitals. There's no trace of the young man. And before you say he probably went off on some kind of jaunt, it would be completely out of character for him to do so. This young man was really looking forward to starting university."

"And your question is. . .?" Allen asked.

"I understand the body found in the church is that of a young man. Could you give me a description?"

"No. We can't release that information before the victim's next-of-kin can be found." Then seeing Maggie's crestfallen face, he added, "But you can give me the description of the missing boy, and I can tell you if it's a match."

Maggie repeated the description Nat had given her over the phone.

Allen, placing a pair of glasses on his nose, drew a buff folder toward him, scanned the first piece of paper then peered at Maggie over the top of his glasses. He shook his head. "Your description does not fit the murder victim. And your second question?"

"The missing boy, Gordon Phelps, was driving a blue 1957 Impala. Do you have any reports of such a vehicle?"

"Do you have the licence number?"

Maggie handed him the slip of paper with the number written on it.

"I'll look into it and let you know," he said, taking it from her. "Are you returning to Naramata now?"

"No." Maggie got up from her chair and turned to leave. "I'm on my way to Summerland to see if the police there have found any trace of the car. I will also call on the Herrmanns—they're the family Gordon Phelps was staying with."

"Good luck! Are you planning on returning to Vancouver soon?"

"Not yet. I'm still on vacation."

He did not look pleased to hear this news.

THE DRIVE TO SUMMERLAND took longer than she had anticipated, mostly because she couldn't resist stopping at the roadside stalls to stock up on fall fruit and jars of honey and preserves. She could see Nat's face—he loved his food—when she unloaded her car on her return home, and suddenly she realized that she was beginning to feel a bit homesick for him.

She found the unpaved Lakeview Road quite easily, but once she had turned onto the downhill track, the glass jars in the trunk rattled together, and she pulled over as close to the edge of the road as she could and stopped the car. She tried not to look down the steep slope to the lake while she concentrated on tucking a spare blanket securely around her purchases. Closing the trunk, she was about to step out to get back behind the wheel when a two-toned, wood-panelled station wagon suddenly barrelled past, narrowly missing her. She stood rooted to the spot as she watched the heavy car speeding around the next bend and out of sight.

Sliding into her seat, she sat for a while to regain her composure. Oscar, feeling her distress, leaned over and gave her a long, wet lick. Maggie laughed and ruffled his head. "I'm okay, Oscar, but am I going to give that . . . that . . . sonofabitch a talking to if I ever catch up with him—or her." She stared down at the lake, glittering in the late afternoon sun with what appeared to be thousands of diamonds. Ducks bobbed up and down on the rippled surface and gulls whirled and swooped, their raucous cries filling the air. Maggie started up the car and continued down Lakeview Road until she came to a T-junction where she swung the car left, hoping it was the right choice.

She was in luck. Number 42, Bide-A-Wee-While Cottage, was the last of the five houses on the lane. A fine gravel path led from the road down to the scuffed front door. On the left side of the house was a garage with its peeling, blue-painted door firmly shut, and the driveway was bereft of cars. Oscar, his head hanging out of the open window on the passenger's side of Maggie's little red car, watched her approach the front door.

The bell didn't seem to work so she rapped sharply on the door, but it was pretty obvious the house was empty, and there didn't seem to be any handy flower pots nearby where a key might have been hidden. Oscar, released from the car, smelled and peed on every sparse blade of grass as he followed Maggie slowly back along the lane, knocking on each door. There was no sign of life in these other houses either, but they were obviously all summer places and the owners or renters were long gone back to the workaday world.

Returning to Bide-a-Wee-While Cottage, she walked determinedly around to the back where a couple of rusty bikes leaned against the wall. There were plenty of flower pots and a few abandoned garden tools—but no sign of a key. A small shed near the back fence held a workbench, a canoe, an assortment of paddles, some fishing rods and three ancient life jackets. Rusty cans sat on a makeshift shelf. She closed the shed door and returned to the back door of the house. "Why didn't I wear proper shoes?" She looked down at her sandaled feet, now filled with wet sand, and leaned against the door to empty each sandal, banging it against the door for good measure before replacing it on her foot. Then instinctively she bent down to pick up the mat she had been standing on to give it a good shake—and there was the errant key.

She could hear Nat's voice telling her that she would be trespassing, but she reasoned that it was possible there could be signs of his client's brother in the cottage and the only way to find out was to go in. She took a Kleenex tissue from her bag and used it to pick up the key and insert it into the lock.

The back door opened into a kitchen/dining room, which was fairly tidy except for a large jar of peanut butter, an open jar of jam, a sticky knife and a very mouldy loaf of bread on one of the counter tops. The dining area was furnished with a large, scarred pine table, six chairs and a sideboard that held an assortment of odd dishes. She

pushed on a partly open door and found it led into the living room, which was furnished in the same shabby man-
ner. A shelf held paperbacks and hard-covered books, and
magazines littered a coffee table where masses of fruit
flies were making a happy meal of a bowl of very over-
ripe peaches. Beside the bowl were a couple of ashtrays
filled with butts and a half-dozen empty beer bottles. As
Maggie gazed around the room, it occurred to her that the
family had suddenly upped and left in a hurry.

Two of the three bedrooms on the second floor rein-
forced her theory of a hasty retreat. The beds were un-
made, the closet doors were open, leaving empty clothes
hangers swinging by their hooks, and towels in the nearby
bathroom hung askew. She surmised that the large front
bedroom facing the road had been occupied by the parents, and the larger of the back bedrooms must have belonged to their son Adam. She opened the closet in that
room and found it full of clothes that obviously belonged
to a young man, and pulling a pair of jeans off a hook, she
held them against her own body. "Too short," she told Oscar. "These don't belong to Gordon."

In the third bedroom the single bed was neatly made,
and opening the closet door, she saw it was crammed with
clothing on hangers. She pawed through them, moving
each garment aside, but it was mainly old raingear and
women's coats. However, at the far end she discovered a
new yellow slicker and a hand-knitted wheat-coloured
sweater. "These could belong to Gordon." She felt in the
pockets of the slicker but found only a roll of sticky candy

and a crumpled handkerchief. But as she was putting it back, she looked down and saw a khaki rucksack.

"Aha! We've found something here, Oscar." She knelt to pick it up.

The dog suddenly gave a low growl.

"What's wrong, Oscar? It's only a bag." But the dog gave another growl and moved toward the door. Maggie got quickly to her feet and grabbed his collar before she peered from the window into the empty back yard. "There's nothing down there." But the dog gave another rumbling growl and pulled her toward the door. Maggie, a firm believer in Oscar's instincts, held onto his collar and tiptoed along the passage into the master bedroom. "Quiet," she whispered as she moved to the window and looked down on the lane below.

She was just in time to see someone—she wasn't sure if it was a man or a woman—slip into the driver's seat of the wood-paneled station wagon that was parked farther up the lane. "It's time for us to be on our way, too," she muttered as she watched the car pull away and disappear up the hill. "But not before I get that rucksack." Going back to the closet, she grabbed it and started for the door again.

Although anxious to get away, she checked the room to make sure she had left everything as she had found it. She had a feeling that whoever owned that station wagon would be back.

IT WAS AFTER SIX before she left Summerland, and as she drove back to Naramata on the unfamiliar roads, she became very tense. She found herself checking again and again in her rear-view mirror for signs of someone following before she realized that she wouldn't know if they were. She was almost back to Apple Orchard Bed and Breakfast when it came to her that she'd completely forgotten to call at the Summerland police station to ask about Gordon's blue Impala. But she had already made a mental list of questions she was going to ask Nat when she telephoned him later.

"We've been so worried about you," Bianca greeted her, giving her a hug. "We thought you were only going to Penticton, but Sergeant Allen called and asked that you get in touch with him when you returned from Summerland. That's when we got worried."

"It looks like we've found your blue Impala," Allen announced when Maggie called the number he'd left for her.

"You have? Can you tell me where?"

"It was on a side road near Kaleden Junction. A Mr. Williamson who has a small holding near there found it. He'd passed it several times before noticing it."

"Was it. . .was it empty?" Maggie asked tentatively.

"There was no one in it if that's what you're asking. But the car's a wreck. Looks like whoever was behind the wheel took the corner too fast, crashed into a rock face and rolled off the road into some bushes. That's why Williamson missed seeing it. Must be the one you're looking for as no one else has reported a missing blue Impala."

"Did they check the licence plates?"

"There were no plates on it."

"But where's Gordon Phelps?"

"Can't help you with that one. But the car could have been pinched by that motorcycle gang—the Red Devil Riders—that have been causing trouble in the valley lately."

"Can you tell me the name of the road where it was found?" Maggie asked, juggling the phone receiver as she retrieved her notebook from her bag.

"The car isn't there now. The Keremeos detachment hauled it to their yard."

"Would it be possible for me to see it?"

"I don't see why not. Give the Keremeos detachment a call." And he gave her the phone number.

After she hung up, she was about to dial Nat's number when Bianca said, "Not until you have something to eat. Your partner can wait another half hour."

Maggie replaced the phone. She was absolutely famished.

CHAPTER NINE

Although Bianca had insisted Maggie call from the telephone in the house, after supper she headed for the telephone booth outside the post office. What she was about to tell Nat had to be kept to themselves for a while.

"Slow down and go through everything again," Nat insisted after she had described her day, starting with learning from Sergeant Allen that the body in the church couldn't be Gordon Phelps.

"But, Nat, where's the Herrmann family? And why does the house in Summerland look as if they left in a hurry? And why was Gordon's knapsack in that closet?"

"I admit this case is getting a bit bizarre," Nat answered. "And, Maggie, I don't need to tell you that you were trespassing."

"And how else would I have found the knapsack and seen the state of the place?"

"I was only teasing you. You know you were expecting me to say that. Now, how sure are you that the knapsack is Gordon's?"

"I won't be until you've spoken to his sister. I'll give you the complete list and you can ask her if she recognizes the items."

"Right! Shoot."

"Blue striped pj's, three pairs Standfield's underwear, blue swimming trunks, white Arrow dress shirt and a couple of T-shirts—one white, one blue—one pair of jeans, four white handkerchiefs, two pairs of white socks, tennis shoes size ten, medium size nylon windbreaker, note book with sketches of boats, apple trees, that kind of stuff. Well drawn. Oh, and a small pair of binoculars."

"Any money?"

"No." She paused for a moment. "Did I tell you about the clothes in his closet? There was a yellow rain-slicker and a cable stitch sweater."

"I'll get onto Fiona right away. Call me back tomorrow, okay? And Maggie," he added seriously, "don't go back to Summerland. I don't like the sound of that station wagon. It could just be someone being nosy and wondering what you were doing at the house, but I've got a nasty feeling about this case."

"Me too. But just one thing more before I hang up—ask Miss Phelps what this Adam Herrmann looks like."

"I know what you're thinking, Maggie—if the body in the church isn't Gordon's, it could possibly be Adam's. And nobody's reported him missing because the parents have disappeared, too. . ."

There was silence on the line before Maggie said, "I'm going to Keremeos to see that Impala tomorrow and then call in on Sergeant Allen again. So it could be late afternoon before I get back to you."

"Please be careful and call me as soon as you get back."

Bianca and Alonso, their rocking chairs moving in unison, were sitting on the porch enjoying the mild evening air when she returned to the guest house.

"Had a nice chat with your young man?" Bianca said, indicating the porch swing.

Maggie laughed. "Neither of us are what you'd call young, Bianca, but yes, we had a good talk." She turned to Alonso. "That young man murdered in the church—don't suppose you know what he looked like?"

Alonso shook his head. "I think Jim maybe see him next day when he goes back with the fire chief." He scratched his head. "Don't remember him saying, though."

Maggie rose to her feet. "Would it be too late for me to walk over and ask?"

"Do you think it might be the boy your partner's trying to find?" Bianca asked.

"It's a long shot," Maggie answered, unwilling to explain they had come to a dead end with that line of inquiry.

"I'll come with you," Bianca said. "I want to ask Marjorie for her peach chutney recipe."

"DIDN'T GET TO SEE very much," Jim Robertson said in answer to Maggie's question. "You see, the coroner and the police were there by the time I got back to the church." He was quiet for a few moments, going over the tragedy in his mind. "I got a glimpse of dark hair as they wrapped him up, but that's about it. Not much help, I'm afraid."

"Maggie wondered if it could be a young man her partner is looking for," Bianca said.

"But what would he be doing here?" Marjorie cut in. "We're a long way from Vancouver."

"This boy had been staying with friends in Summerland," Maggie explained. "He didn't return home when he was expected, and we can't find the family he was staying with."

"Even so, it would be very unlikely for him to turn up in Naramata," Jim said. "I mean, how would he have got here from Summerland? He'd need a car, wouldn't he?"

"Maybe he was brought here by the man who murdered him?" Bianca suggested.

"Now that's possible," Marjorie said. "Or he could have come over here by boat," she added excitedly. "It wouldn't take that long to get here."

"But someone along the shore there would have heard a boat motor," Bianca said.

"But what was he doing in our church?" Jim said.

"That's what I mean," Bianca chimed in. Then she turned to Maggie and grinned. "You'll make detectives out of us yet."

"Suppose the murderer is someone living right here in Naramata?" Marjorie said with a shiver. "Suppose it's someone we know?"

"Why don't you go and talk to Sergeant Allen in the morning?" Jim advised. "He could give you a description of the dead man."

"A good idea," Maggie replied. There was no point in admitting she had already asked the sergeant that very question and been turned down.

When they arrived back at the guest house, Bianca insisted on making Maggie a hot chocolate. "This will give you a good sleep," she said, popping a couple of marshmallows into the cup before pouring the hot chocolate into it. "Being a detective is quite exhausting, isn't it?"

CHAPTER TEN

The Impala was in poor shape, which wasn't surprising considering it had skidded into the side road—apparently at excessive speed—bounced off a rocky outcrop then rolled over a cliff to come to rest amid a clump of greasewood. The RCMP officer told Maggie that several people had heard the screeching of tires and the crash in the middle of the night, but they didn't locate the car until a couple of days later. The strangest thing about it, he said, was that there were no licence plates on the car when it was found, so they'd been unable to track down the owner. However, if she could supply them with some kind of identification and the owner's name, they would be only too happy for her to arrange to have it towed away.

"As you can see, we barely have enough room for our two squad cars here," he added as he led her back into the police station.

"I'm afraid the young man who owns the car has gone missing," she explained, handing over her PI card. "My partner, Nat Southby, has been retained by the family to find him, and the trail seems to have stopped in Summerland."

"And he's sent you all the way from Vancouver to look at the car?"

"No. I happened to be on vacation in the Valley."

"That's rather a lucky coincidence," he said scathingly, handing her card back to her. "Perhaps you'd better fill me in on the rest of the story."

So Maggie spent the next twenty minutes repeating the saga of Gordon Phelps' disappearance. But although she told the constable where the Herrmann's house was located in Summerland, she didn't bother to mention that she had gone inside it, and she didn't tell him about the station wagon—or the knapsack. After all, these things could be just coincidences.

AT THE PENTICTON RCMP station when Maggie asked to see Sergeant Allen, the desk officer asked, "Is the sergeant expecting you?"

"Would you see if he's available?" she said, giving the man one of her most winning smiles.

"He's very busy. What's it about?"

But Sergeant Allen was already standing in the open doorway to his office. "Mrs. Spencer," he said. "You been to see the Impala?"

Maggie nodded. "I wonder if I could speak to you for a moment?"

He peered up at the large wall clock. "I can give you exactly ten minutes. Come in."

He didn't invite her to sit, just looked at her expectantly.

"Have you identified the body in the church yet?"

"No. Why?"

"I know it isn't our client's brother. But Gordon Phelps was staying with a friend named Adam Herrmann who is about the same age, and we can't seem to locate him either—or his parents."

Allen sighed wearily and moved behind his desk. "You might as well sit down. What does this young man look like and why would he be in Naramata?"

"Well. . . well, actually I don't have his description yet. I'm waiting to hear from my partner. But when I was in Summerland yesterday, I discovered that there is no one in the house where Gordon stayed."

"So you decided that since the Phelps boy's car ended up in Kaleden Junction, the dead man in the Naramata church must be this Adam Herrmann. That's a bit of a stretch, isn't it?"

Maggie felt herself blushing. "No, Sergeant, I'm just doing regular detective work." She stood up and started for the door.

"Mrs. Spencer."

She turned back. "Yes?"

"We know how the fire started."

"You do? How?"

"It was apparently started by a cigarette butt in the waste paper basket in the rector's office. The drapes caught fire and it went straight up the wall to the roof because the wood inside that old church was tinder dry."

Maggie didn't tell the sergeant that this bit of information had already been given to her by one of the volunteer firemen. Instead she asked, "And that's why the rafters collapsed into the church?"

Allen nodded. "Those heavy beams fell and toppled the pulpit, and as luck would have it, the pulpit covered the body and prevented it being burned to a cinder."

Maggie nodded thoughtfully. "Georgina Jennings says she saw the man in the cloak running away quite some time *before* the fire was discovered. So if he is the murderer, he left before making sure that his victim would be completely burned along with the church."

"So we struck it lucky," Allen said.

"You know, of course," Maggie said, "there's no way the man in the cloak was Mr. Schultz."

She caught a glimmer of a smile on Allen's face before he answered her. "And what's your reason for deciding that he's innocent?"

"Karl Schultz isn't in any condition to run away from anything—espccially a fire."

"You mean that walking stick? He could be faking."

"Come off it, Sergeant. You and I have both interviewed the man. He's not faking. And there's one more thing—the fire destroyed the church organ."

"And you figure that an organist would not willfully destroy an instrument that he loved." He walked past her to the door and opened it for her. "Call me when you have a description of this Adam Herrmann."

NAT WAS WAITING IMPATIENTLY for her call. "I was getting worried."

"Nat, Keremeos isn't exactly around the corner from Naramata. And the police there wanted to know all the particulars about the owner of the car and then the missing person case we're investigating. I'm sure the car is Gordon's, but I'm afraid that his sister will have to come to Keremeos to identify it."

"I'll tell her," Nat answered. "Anyway, you wanted Adam's description. Fiona says she only saw him a couple of times but she thinks he's nearly the same height as her brother—around 5' 11", sort of muscular, dark hair—almost black—brown eyes, slightly crooked nose—she remembers Gordon telling her that he's done some amateur boxing—and he dresses well."

Maggie promised him she would call as soon as she had spoken to the sergeant again. "Are you going to drive her to Keremeos to see the car?" she asked.

"Wasn't planning to," Nat answered. "The Blackthorn accident case is still dragging on, and we haven't made much progress with that Sowerby fraud investigation. One of the principals is obviously lying, and George is convinced it's our client!"

"I wouldn't be surprised if he wasn't right! That guy seemed a bit shifty to me. But I'm sure you'll get a break soon," she assured him. "How are George and Henny getting along?"

"I think George is getting fed up with burnt cookies. I found some buried deep in the waste-paper basket yesterday."

They both laughed.

THE SERGEANT WAS JUST about to leave his office when Maggie phoned him.

"What now, Mrs. Spencer?"

"I have the description of Adam Herrmann."

There was a few seconds of silence after Maggie finished, then he said, "And if I understood you right, you haven't been able to locate the parents."

"Which, considering the circumstances and if your John Doe is the missing boy," Maggie answered, "does seem a bit odd, don't you think?"

"I'm not saying our body is your missing man, but would your partner's client be able to identify him?"

"Probably," Maggie answered. "She met him a couple of times with her brother, and she's coming to Keremeos to identify the car."

"Any idea when that will be?"

"No. But I imagine it will be sometime in the next couple of days."

"I think I'd better call Mr. Southby myself. I've got your business card and I guess his number's the same as yours, eh?"

"That's a very good idea, Sergeant. But he's probably gone home for the day, so you'll need his home phone. . ."

CHAPTER ELEVEN

George Sawasky, balancing a cup of coffee in one hand and a file in the other, settled into the chair across from Nat. "You wanted to see me, boss?" he asked, smiling.

"I had a phone call from this Sergeant Allen in Penticton last night. He wants Fiona Phelps to call into the station to see if she can identify the body they've got."

"He doesn't think it's Gordon Phelps, does he?"

Nat shook his head. "The description doesn't tally. But it could possibly be this Adam Herrmann, and Fiona met him a couple of times so it's possible she could identify him."

"Have you told her yet?"

"Called her first thing this morning and she'll be here around nine. But she wants me to go with her."

"Are you going?"

"To be honest, George, I don't think I can spare the time with all we've got on our plate right now."

"But you don't have much choice, have you? She's your client."

"But it would be too much of a coincidence for Maggie's corpse and that torched church to be linked to Adam Herrmann and Gordon Phelps."

"True. But you know how often coincidences happen in this business. And if the body should prove to be Adam

Herrmann, and Gordon was staying with him just before he disappeared . . ?"

"Yeah, you're right. It would give us a fresh lead." Nat suddenly grinned. "But what's Maggie going to say? Especially after me telling her to leave the murder to the local cops?"

"She'll rag you a bit. But I think Maggie will be kinda pleased to see you." He grinned, stood up prepared to leave the office then turned back. "It's none of my business, Nat, but why the hell don't you two tie the knot? You obviously love each other . . ."

Nat looked up, surprised. "Oh, I thought you knew. . . " And he proceeded to explain how Harry Spencer refused to risk his reputation as a respected lawyer to give Maggie what he called "a dirty divorce."

"But he must want to get on with his own life, find somebody else to marry. It must be at least five years since she left him . . ."

"Just four. . . It happened right after the Chandler case." When George looked puzzled, Nat continued, "You remember Shadow Lake?"

"Oh right. Near Horsefly. The place where you fell down the mine shaft. Of course I remember." He was silent for a moment. "And that's where I met Harry."

"Harry? What was Harry doing there?"

"It was when you were in Williams Lake hospital and I came up there to help Maggie. Harry turned up one day, demanding she come home right now or else . . . He's an unpleasant character, isn't he?"

"I'm glad I was out of it or I would've punched him in the nose."

"I nearly did! Anyhow, you can't tell me he hasn't been up to a little hanky-panky of his own since then."

"Apparently not. He's still determined Maggie's going to come back to him."

"And she's not, is she?"

"My god, I hope not!"

"Well then, you'd better get up to the Okanagan, eh?"

"Do you think you'll be able to carry the ball here on your own?" Nat turned the flip calendar on his desk to face George. "Tomorrow's Friday and I can't see us being there more than a couple of days."

"I'll give it my best." He grinned. "After all, I'll have Henny to keep me on the straight and narrow. But," he continued, "I think you'd better be prepared to be there more than a couple of days."

"YOU ARE ACTUALLY COMING HERE?" Maggie said incredulously. "I don't believe it! And after all those lectures." She laughed. "So what's the plan?"

"Fiona Phelps is driving. We'll stop in Keremeos to see the Impala, and we hope to arrive at the Penticton RCMP detachment late tomorrow afternoon. Allen says he'll take us straight to the morgue at the hospital."

"Where will you stay?"

"We've booked rooms for the night at a local motel."

"Good idea. I would ask Bianca but she only has two guest rooms. . ."

"And she wouldn't approve if I moved in with you. . ."

"They only know that I'm separated and that I'm a partner at Southby and Spencer Investigations. As it is," she added, "they have a hard time understanding how a woman could be a detective."

Nat laughed. "Guess I'll just have to smuggle you into my motel room."

"Call me as soon as you arrive."

"YOU BRING YOUR BOSS and his client here for supper," Bianca said when Maggie explained what was happening.

"I'm afraid they'll arrive too late for supper, but perhaps on Saturday? I would really like you to meet Nat."

"Ah-ha! Is he married?"

Maggie laughed. "No."

"Then he is too old for you?"

"We're the same age."

"I see!" Bianca nodded sagely then repeated, "You bring him and the poor lady who's lost her brother for dinner on Saturday."

MAGGIE GLANCED AT HER watch again. As promised, Nat had called at 5:30 to say that he and Fiona Phelps had arrived at their motel. After a quick freshen-up, he said, they would be on their way to the morgue, and they would meet Maggie at the Lakeside Restaurant around seven. But it was now past the half hour.

"Are you ready to order?" Pen and pad in hand, the elderly waitress hovered impatiently over Maggie.

"Just bring me another coffee. Hopefully my friends should be here shortly."

The waitress sniffed. "We close at nine, you know."

Maggie, who had placed herself facing the door, looked up as it opened once again. This time an exhausted auburn-haired woman walked through it, followed by an equally exhausted Nat. The woman stood uncertainly just inside the doorway until Nat took her by the elbow and steered her toward Maggie.

"Oh, here they are," Maggie told the waitress.

She plonked three menus on the table. "You still want that coffee?" she demanded.

"Yes. But come back in a few minutes." She stood up to greet them.

"Fiona, this is Maggie, my partner."

"I'm so pleased to meet you, Miss Phelps, but sorry it's under these circumstances." Maggie held out her hand. "You both look absolutely done-in. Sit down and I'll order you a coffee."

"I don't know about you, Nat," Fiona said as Nat pulled out a chair for her, "but I could do with a straight Scotch."

"That'll be the day when one can order liquor in a res-taurant! But I see by the sign outside that they do serve beer, so I'll have a cold one, though not until I've greeted my partner properly." Fiona looked slightly surprised as

Nat went round to Maggie's chair, pulled her to her feet again and gave her a smacking kiss. "Now we can order."

Maggie, slightly pink in the face, beckoned the surly waitress over. After they had ordered dinner and Nat's beer, she asked, "Were you able to identify the body in the morgue, Miss Phelps?"

"Please call me Fiona. Yes. Thankfully it wasn't my brother, but I'm pretty sure it's Adam Herrmann. I only met him a couple of times, but I'm sure it's him. But it only makes Gordon's disappearance even scarier. Where can he be?"

"Did you stop in Keremeos to see the car?"

Fiona nodded. "It's Gordon's car all right." She sat quietly for a moment. "But I can't understand why there were no licence plates on it or why they found it where they did and why there was no sign of him there. And how come Adam was found dead in church miles away from where he was staying with his parents? And where are his parents?"

Neither Nat nor Maggie had answers to her questions, and they sat in silence for a moment before Maggie asked, "Are you having the car towed home?"

"I intended to, but the RCMP in Keremeos won't release it now because there could be a connection with Adam's murder."

"Fiona wants to go to the Herrmanns' house in Summerland," Nat said. "What about first thing in the morning?"

Maggie nodded. "I'll pick you up around nine. Hopefully, as you've only just identified the victim, the police won't have the place cordoned off yet."

GEORGE SAWASKY PARKED DOWN the street from the bus stop, unfolded his newspaper and peered over the top of it. The bus arrived minutes later and he watched his quarry alight then raised his newspaper a little higher as a dark blue Chrysler Windsor pulled up. He watched his quarry slip into the passenger seat before the car proceeded north. George lowered his newspaper, started his engine and followed. When the Chrysler finally parked outside the hotel, he remained in his car watching the pair enter.

It was going to be another long night. He opened his thermos and poured himself a cup of coffee.

CHAPTER TWELVE

A few rain drops sneaked down the dusty windshield of the red Morris Minor as Maggie left the Rinaldis' house for Penticton the following morning. There wasn't enough rain to use her wipers, and she considered stopping to deal with the smears, but she was running late—Bianca had insisted she have a proper breakfast—and dust from the unpaved road ahead would only make the glass dirty again.

"For god's sake, rain if you're going to," she muttered in exasperation at the ominous clouds overhead. Her answer was a flash of lightning followed by a roll of thunder travelling down the valley. Oscar, sitting on the back seat, buried his head under the sweater she'd left there. She glanced at her watch. *Nat will be wondering where I am.*

At that moment a familiar-looking station wagon materialized out of one of the orchard driveways in front of her, and she slammed on the brakes and came to a shuddering stop. Heart thumping, for a brief moment she rested her head on the wheel, and when she looked up again, she was just in time to see the station wagon gathering speed as it disappeared around the next bend in the road.

Where the hell did that damned thing come from? But the horn beeping behind her told her that she was holding up a truck laden with bins full of apples, and she put her car into gear and set off again. When she rounded the bend, there was no sign of the station wagon. *Must have turned off into one of these orchards,* she told herself, but though she peered down each driveway, she didn't see it again.

BY THE TIME NAT and Fiona finished their coffee and Danish in the tiny café adjoining their motel, the skies had opened up and the rain was beating on the roof.

"Is Summerland far?" Fiona asked anxiously as she watched the rain dancing in the puddles on the road outside.

Nat shook his head then glanced at his watch. "Unusual for Maggie to be late," he muttered. "Would you like another coffee?"

"No thanks," Fiona said. "I'll just slip into the washroom while we wait for her."

She had no sooner left when the door of the café opened and Maggie stepped inside.

"We were wondering where you'd . . ," Nat said as he rose and started toward her. But he stopped in mid-sentence and put his arm around her. "What's wrong?" he asked as he led her to the table. "Here, sit down and I'll get you some coffee." He beckoned to the waitress.

"Just a little scare. It's probably nothing."

"You look as if it was more than a little scare."

"No. I'm fine. It's probably my imagination playing tricks," and she told him what had just happened. "But there has to be more than one wood-panelled station wagon in the Okanagan Valley," she added.

"I'm sure there is," he answered comfortingly, but neither of them was comforted. "Here's Fiona." As their client rejoined them, he said, "If it's okay with you, Fiona, we'll take your car. Maggie has had a bit of a fright."

"But Oscar's with me," Maggie objected.

"Who is Oscar?" Fiona asked.

"My dog."

"Oscar won't be any trouble," Nat said. "In any case, your car is bigger, Fiona, and Maggie's is a bit too conspicuous." He turned back to Maggie. "You finish your coffee while I settle up with the waitress."

"What happened?" Fiona asked as she watched Nat talking to the waitress at the front counter.

Maggie had just finished providing a brief explanation of the station wagon incident when she saw Nat was holding the café door open for them. "We can park your car behind the motel, Maggie," he said. Five minutes later Nat, driving Fiona's 1960 black Ford Fairlane, pulled cautiously out from behind the motel, and Maggie, sitting in the rear seat with Oscar, leaned as far back as she could into the comfort of the soft leather seat to make sure she was not seen. The street was fairly busy with cars, shoppers and late season tourists, but there was no sign of the station wagon.

"You'll have to direct me," Nat called back to her.

"Just keep the lake on your right and head north."

By the time they reached the small town of Summerland, the rain had stopped and steam was rising from the cedar-shake roofs of the houses that lined the roads. When they came to the T-junction on Lakeview Lane, Maggie leaned forward and, pointing to the left, said, "It's the last house." Unlike her first visit, this time there were cars parked outside several of the houses.

"No sign of the police," Nat said, but instead of proceeding down the street to the Herrmanns' house, he turned the car into the access lane at the top of the street and stopped under a cluster of pines. "We can walk along the beach—just in case your friends in the station wagon are still checking up on you."

They climbed out of the car, and as they skirted a sand dune to reach the beach, Fiona asked, "Do you think the people in that car are the ones who killed Gordon's friend?"

"I wish I knew," Maggie answered. "Hold on a minute, Nat." Slipping her sandals off, she bent and picked them up. "That's better." She smiled up at him as he took her other hand and gave it a gentle squeeze. Oscar, freed from the strange car, loped happily ahead, stopping briefly to greet some children playing ball on the beach, though every now and then he would turn just to make sure Maggie was still following.

A weathered and rickety wood-paled fence separated the Herrmann property from the beach, and small sand dunes sprouting tufts of grass leaned against it, the grass waving its dried fronds in the sudden breeze that had come up as the sun disappeared once again behind scudding clouds. The place was eerily quiet. From this far end of the beach, even the voices of the children they had passed earlier were muted. Maggie felt ominous shudders run up her spine as huge drops of rain began splattering down. As she paused to put on her shoes again, Nat swung the gate open and led the way up the gravel path to the back of the house.

Behind her she heard Fiona say, "Is this it? Somehow I thought it would be . . ." she paused, "in. . . in better shape. Gordon rhapsodized about the place."

"These summer places always look miserable on days like this," Nat said as cheerfully as he could. "Let's get under the eaves before it really rains. Maggie, when you were here before, did you have a look in that shed?" He pointed at the small shed they had passed close to the back fence.

She nodded. "There's nothing much in there except an old canoe, some paddles and stuff like that—the usual summer cottage junk."

"Is there any way we can get inside the house?" Fiona asked.

Maggie was beginning to find Fiona's whining voice a bit irritating. "There was a key under the mat last time I was here. If you move over, I'll see if it's still there." It was, and Maggie looked up enquiringly at Nat.

"Okay, but let's be quick about it. And, Fiona, please don't touch anything. We don't want to mix our fingerprints with whoever was here before us." He turned back to Maggie, "I hope you were careful when you were here bef. . ."

"Of course," she answered shortly. She had already pulled a couple of Kleenex tissues from her pocket, one to pick up the key, the other to use on the door knob.

Nat had the grace to look slightly ashamed for questioning her knowledge of correct procedure.

"What's that dreadful smell?" Fiona said as they entered the kitchen.

"It's that bowl of fruit in the living room," Maggie answered. As the fruit had now decomposed to a brown sodden mess, there were even more fruit flies than before hovering over it.

Screwing up her face in disgust, Fiona started toward it. "I'll empty it into the garbage," she said.

"No!" Nat snapped. "Don't touch it! The police are going to be taking fingerprints here and we don't want them asking what you were doing here, do we?"

Somewhat affronted, Fiona said primly, "We have such a lovely home in Vancouver. Why would Gordon enjoy a place like this?" She waved a hand at the dowdy, mismatched furniture and the offensive bowl of fruit.

Maybe to get away from you, Maggie thought, though she had to admit that the grey light of the rainy day filtering through the thin drapes partly drawn over the front windows made the place look even more depressing than on her first visit. "I guess you'd like to see Gordon's room, Fiona," she said lightly and led the way out of the living room and up the narrow staircase. "I'm pretty sure this is the one he used," she added. "Is he usually so neat and tidy?"

Fiona nodded. "Yes, very." She ran her hands over the neatly made bed. "His grandfather. . ." She paused. "His father was in the army and taught him to do square corners." She straightened and, turning, caught sight of the sweater hanging in the closet. "And that's Gordon's sweater! I knitted it for him." And before Maggie had time to stop her, she had grabbed it out of the closet and was burying her nose in it. "Do you think it would be okay if I take it back with me?"

"No. I'm sorry, Fiona," Nat said from the doorway, "but it has to stay right there in the closet. Please put it back *exactly* as you found it."

"But no one will know. . ."

"Fiona," Maggie said gently, taking the sweater and putting it back on its hanger, "whoever else was here will know it's missing. And that reminds me, did that rucksack belong to your brother?" She had passed the bag over to Nat the previous evening.

"Yes. I bought it for him to take on this trip. Did you look at his sketch book?" she asked proudly. "He is such a good artist."

"Sketchbook?" Nat asked sharply.

"Yes," Fiona answered. "He always carries one with him. I took him for a holiday in Mexico when he was ten and he filled two books with his sketches. He would just go up to people and ask if he could draw them. By the time we came home, he had two whole books of people and places and—"

"I think I'd better look through it when we return to the motel," Nat interrupted. "Are you finished here?"

But Fiona's face had crumpled and she looked forlornly around the room. "What I can't understand is why his car was found abandoned on that road so far from here. And where are the licence plates?" And she sat on the bed and began to cry. "He's been murdered, too, hasn't he?"

"We don't know that, Fiona," Nat answered quietly from the doorway. "But I think we should be on our way before the cops get here."

Maggie helped Fiona to her feet and propelled her gently toward the bedroom door then went back to smooth the blankets on the bed.

"Did you look in the garage, Maggie?" Nat asked once they were outside again.

"No. There wasn't time." She shuddered. "Nat, I think we should go." She was suddenly anxious for them to get as far from the place as possible.

"A quick look," Nat insisted.

Maggie nodded. "Just a quick one."

To their surprise the garage was unlocked and a blue Buick LeSabre four-door sedan sat in the middle of it. However, the car's doors were locked, and although Nat slipped back into the house, hoping to find a spare set of keys, he was out of luck.

"Please let's get out of here," Maggie urged. "The RCMP could turn up here anytime, especially now that Fiona has identified Adam's body."

"You're right. We'll go back the way we came along the beach." Nat closed the garage door and followed Maggie and Fiona to the back of the house. "You two carry on—I'm going to have a look in that shed. I'll catch up to you."

"Oh, do hurry, Nat. Come along, Oscar." The dog ran ahead, and she pushed Fiona through the gate and set off at a brisk pace along the beach, with Fiona half-running to keep up. Although it could only have been a few minutes before Maggie glanced back and saw Nat leaving the property, it seemed an eternity.

"As you said, it's just the usual summer cottage stuff," he said as he caught up to them. It was now raining in earnest, the children had all gone home, and just as they arrived at the narrow beach access where Nat had parked Fiona's car, a police cruiser drove past, heading for the Herrmann house.

"Phew! That was close," Nat said as he slid behind the wheel of Fiona's car.

Maggie, leaning back in the rear seat, agreed. Oscar, snuggled down on his blanket, laid his head on her lap and gave a sigh—he wasn't all that fond of rain.

"COULD YOU TAKE ME to see the church?" Fiona asked as they neared Penticton.

Maggie leaned forward in her seat. "It's pretty well gutted," she said, hoping to dissuade her.

"I'd still like to see it." She was silent for a few moments. "I'm sorry that Adam is dead but so relieved it wasn't my Gordon lying on that slab."

My Gordon! Maggie's mind went back to showing Fiona the room that Gordon had used, and her referring to his *grandfather* teaching him to make square corners. *A slip of the tongue?*

"I'll pick up my car," Maggie said as they approached the motel. "You can follow me to Naramata to see the church. Which reminds me," she added, "Bianca, my hostess, has invited you both for supper tonight. Apart from Bianca being a fantastic cook, I thought you'd like to meet her and her family and see the place where I'm staying. It's really beautiful."

THE RUINED CHURCH WAS now surrounded by police caution tape, and they stood on the nearby sidewalk in the rain gazing at it. "Whatever was Adam doing here?" Fiona said. "And why was he killed in such a horrible way?"

"Did you know the dead boy?" a gruff voice asked. The three of them had been so engrossed that they hadn't heard the man come up behind them. "I heard you say Adam. Did you know . . ." Then as Maggie turned, he recognized her. "Oh, it's Mrs. Spencer, isn't it? We met the other day, didn't we?"

"Nice to see you again." Maggie turned to Nat and Fiona. "This is Anthony Bicknell, St. Martin's rector."

"To answer your question," Fiona said after they'd shaken hands, "No, thank God. . ." Then she blushed. ". . . I mean, I'm sorry that Adam was killed but thankful it wasn't my brother. He was on holiday here with Adam, you see. . ."

"They were about the same age?"

"Yes. They went to high school together. . ."

Anthony Bicknell pointed toward the single-storied house next to the remains of the church. "Could I interest you folks in a cup of coffee? I live right there," he said, "and I've just made a fresh pot. . ."

"We'd love to," Nat said, eager to get out of the rain.

"Follow me then," he said as he led them to the side door of the house and into a large, bright and airy kitchen. A braided rug was set under a maple-wood table with six matching chairs, and in front of a wood stove that crack- led invitingly were two rocking chairs.

"The housekeeper has left enough sandwiches for my lunch to feed an army," Anthony Bicknell said, waving a hand at the waxed paper-covered platter on the table. "And I see she even baked some chocolate chip cookies. Please help yourselves." And he began setting out cups on the table. "Sorry I don't have cream for the coffee, but the housekeeper doesn't think it's good for me." And he laughed ruefully.

"We can't take your lunch," Maggie protested. But Nat, having missed his mid-day meal, was happy to oblige.

"I beg you to help me out," Bicknell said and opened the refrigerator to show them the packed shelves. "Since the fire my parishioners have arrived in a steady parade with casseroles, pies and cakes."

The coffee he provided was surprisingly good, but Maggie knew the rector had an ulterior purpose in inviting them in. "This is really kind of you, Reverend Bicknell, but I think you invited us in because you have something to tell us about the boys . . ." She estimated that the rector must be no more than in his late fifties, and though not a tall man, he was a commanding presence with his grey-streaked hair and steel-blue eyes. He wasn't wearing a wedding ring, though that didn't mean a thing as it was only just becoming popular for a man to wear one. But then he had referred to his housekeeper, not his wife . . .

"Please call me Tony," he said. "Yes, you're right. You see, I think they were the same young men I saw a few days before the fire. I remember them particularly because they were a lot younger than most of the tourists who want to see inside the church, and the taller one had flaming red hair . . ."

"That was Gordon!" Fiona cried out. "Did you speak to him?"

"Briefly. They seemed like a nice couple of lads and both very polite. They looked around the church, asked a few questions about its history then took off."

Maggie couldn't help smiling at the word *lads*. It reminded her of her father who had always referred to teenaged boys as lads.

"Did Gordon say if he was in trouble?" Fiona demanded. "Did he say what he was doing here?" She turned to Nat. "You see I was right. Something awful has happened to him. You have to do something!"

Nat realized that it was useless to tell the woman to keep calm. "Fiona, I grant you that something awful has happened to Gordon's friend," he said slowly, "but there's no evidence that your brother has suffered the same fate."

"But where is he?" she cried.

"Did they have a car?" Nat asked Tony Bicknell.

"No. They said they'd rowed across the lake from Summerland."

Nat turned to Maggie, "Do you remember seeing a rowboat at the cottage?"

"No, there was just that canoe in the shed. And they would have said *paddled* if they had come over here by canoe. But wait a minute, there were some oars standing up in the corner with all those paddles, so there must have been a rowboat around there at some time . . ."

"About those two boys," Nat said, turning back to the rector, "I don't suppose you remember the exact day you spoke to them?"

"I might be able to . . ." Tony Bicknell rose from his chair and walked to the telephone table to pick up his day diary. "I'm only in Naramata from Sunday evening until Wednesday each week," he explained as he turned the pages, "and I'm always tied up with Boy Scouts on Wednesday, so it was either Monday or Tuesday. I tend to think it was Tuesday. . . around noon. Yes, I'm sure that's it—Mrs. Davies usually cleans the place when I'm not here, but this last week she came on Tuesday, and that vacuum makes such an awful racket that I went over to the church to work in my office. Is that any help to you?"

Nat nodded. "A great help. It tells us they were still around here five days before the fire."

"But Gordon knew he had to be back the day after Labour Day!" Fiona said, and then turning to Tony Bicknell, she explained, "He's starting his first year at UBC this fall."

"I'm so sorry I can't be of more help," he replied, patting her shoulder. "Do the parents of the other boy know he's dead?"

"Unfortunately, the police haven't been able to locate them," Maggie answered, getting up from the table. "But we must be going. Thank you so much for the coffee."

"And the lunch," Nat added around a mouthful of chocolate chip cookie.

They were at the side door when Maggie turned back to him, "You're originally from the West Country, aren't you?"

He laughed. "It still shows in my accent, eh? My dear wife and I emigrated from Wiltshire more than twenty-five years ago."

It was on the tip of Maggie's tongue to ask if he was recently widowed, when he continued, "I know she would have loved to have met a fellow Brit—you're from Kent, aren't you?" he said, beaming at Maggie, "but she's on duty at the Kelowna hospital over the weekend."

"A nurse?" Fiona asked.

"A doctor," he answered proudly. "And she's very well thought of there." He chuckled. "We're a great team—she looks after their bodies and I take care of their souls—well, at least I hold up my end of it there from Thursday to Sunday each week." He smiled at Fiona. "And my dear, I'm always here if you need me."

Fiona was fitting the key into the door of her car before she muttered, "As if I would bare my problems to that do-gooder." Then she directed herself to Maggie: "What time is your landlady expecting us?"

"Make it around five," Maggie answered. "And if you follow my car, I'll show you the turn-off leading to their place."

As Nat walked Maggie to her car, he noted the tight set of her lips and said, "Be patient with her, Maggie. She's worried about her brother."

"Her son, you mean," she answered shortly. "Don't be late for supper."

CHAPTER THIRTEEN

That evening Bianca outdid herself. The table was laden with antipasti, pasta, sauces and cheeses, chicken and vegetables and crusty home-made bread, all washed down with Alonso's own wines.

"Bianca," Nat said, leaning back in his chair as she placed a large wedge of apple pie in front of him, "this is absolutely wonderful. No wonder Maggie wants to stay here forever."

"We would love to have her stay," she said, smiling back at him, "but something tells me she misses a certain someone." As she served pie to Fiona, she said, "We are so sorry about your brother, Miss Phelps. But Maggie is very clever—she will find him. Look how she cleared Karl Schulz's name? The police say they now believe him and it is someone unknown who set the fire."

"As long as they don't think it was my brother who did it," Fiona said in an aggrieved voice.

"Why would they think that?" Alonso asked.

"We spoke to Reverend Bicknell this afternoon," Maggie explained, "and just a few days prior to the fire, two boys matching Gordon and Adam's description asked if they could see inside the church."

"But that doesn't mean they set the fire," Alonso said.

"But why did they want to see inside?" Bianca asked.

"That's the reason they're suspect," Maggie said. "Especially since Adam was killed there a few days later."

"Your parents must be worried sick that their son is still missing." Bianca's eyes filled with tears as she looked across the table at her own son busily mopping up his plate.

Fiona looked confused for a moment then said, "Yes. My father is still insisting that Gordon has just gone off with a friend somewhere."

"He doesn't know about the car being found then?" Alonso asked, passing a bowl of whipped cream to her.

"No." Fiona took a small spoonful of the cream, plopped it onto the pie in front of her and passed the bowl to Maggie. "You see, they are very elderly. I haven't told them yet." And picking up her dessert fork, she broke into the flakey pastry.

Maggie glanced at Nat but he was studiously avoiding her gaze.

"HOW LONG DO YOU STAY?" Alonso asked Nat as they carried their coffee to the porch.

Nat glanced uneasily at Maggie as he took the seat beside her on the porch swing. "I have to be back in Vancouver by noon Monday," he told Alonso. "Our assistant is very new to the job and there have been some complications in our other cases."

"How are you getting back?" Maggie asked.

"There's an early bus from Penticton. Fiona wants to stay here in case there's news about Gordon, and I thought that, since you're already here, Maggie. . ." His voice faded.

"Do you intend coming back?" Maggie asked icily.

"Of course! But I've got to straighten out a few things with George on the Blackthorn case, and he's making arrangements for us to see Adam's uncle, Wilhelm Herrmann, on Monday afternoon. We're hoping by talking to him face to face he'll be a little more open about where the hell the boy's parents have got to."

"Why didn't your assistant go and see him today?" Fiona demanded.

When Nat explained that George could not be asked to work on weekends, Fiona gave a snort of disgust, put down her coffee cup and headed for her car.

A little later as Maggie and Nat walked to Fiona's car, he took her hand. "You do understand?" he asked. A wind had arisen and the leaves of the apple trees rustled all around them. "It's not fair to leave George dealing with both the Blackthorn and Sowerby investigations all by himself . . ."

Maggie shivered. "Of course," she admitted, "but I just wish you'd told me your plans earlier."

"Didn't have a chance. And, by the way, you were right."

"About what?"

"Fiona is Gordon's mother."

"She told you?"

"On the way here I insisted that her parents had a right to know about finding his car, and she broke down and told me. It was a teenage pregnancy. She refused to have him adopted out, so they agreed to bring him up as theirs while she continued her schooling."

"Will you be seeing them?"

"Yes, as soon as I get back." He pulled her tighter towards him. "But we still have tomorrow together."

"Can we have it without Fiona?"

He grinned. "Pick me up in the morning." Bending down, he gave her a quick kiss.

"Have you had a look at Gordon's sketch book?"

"No. Why?"

"Just a hunch. Ask Fiona if you can borrow it and bring it with you in the morning."

"What about slipping back to the Herrmanns' house and having a look inside that shed?"

Maggie laughed. "So we're going to have a day off together, are we?"

NEXT MORNING MAGGIE PARKED her Morris Minor discreetly beneath the stunted pines in the beach access lane. "Did Fiona give you the sketchbook?" she asked as they climbed out of the car. Fortunately, Fiona had announced the night before that she intended to sleep late, so they had been able to slip away without her.

Nat opened the car's back door to let an excited Oscar out onto the sand. "Yeah, she gave it to me, but I'm not sure why you want it as he seems to have just drawn the usual things you'd see on vacation in a place like this—

water, beaches, beach houses, boats—plus a couple of sketches of someone I take to be Adam."

"Can I see it?"

"Now? It's in my knapsack."

She held out her hand. "Just a quick look before we head along the beach."

Grumbling under his breath, he placed his rucksack on the sand and proceeded to unload its contents. First a packet of stale sandwiches, then a thermos and a pair of binoculars followed by spare socks, a crumpled handkerchief and a hand towel—obviously from the motel—and finally the sketch book, which he handed to Maggie. The smell of the sandwiches brought Oscar scuttling back to where they were standing, and before Nat could stop him, the dog was burying his nose into the bag as Nat struggled to put the items back.

"They're not for you, Oscar," he yelled, pushing the dog away. "Scram!"

Maggie, already immersed in the sketchbook, was immune to the struggle between man and dog. The drawings were well done, and she could see why Fiona was proud of her son. "Look here, Nat. This is the front of the Herrmanns' beach house, and the next page shows the back yard and then there's two sketches of the inside of that shed."

His rucksack safely back in the car, Nat peered over her shoulder at the drawings. "I told you that shed needs a thorough going-over." He pointed to a detail in one of the shed drawings. "I wonder why they have that piece of carpet on the middle of the floor."

"M-m-m. And I wonder why he made such a meticulous drawing of it." She riffled through the rest of the pages, which showed other buildings and places, though none in such detail. "We need more time to really look at this book, but I have a gut feeling that he was doing his best to record everything as carefully as he could. I'll keep it in my bag, okay?"

"Fine with me."

As they started their walk along the beach, Maggie pulled her cardigan tighter. It wasn't raining this morning, but the sun was often obscured by clouds, and the cool wind that rippled through the tall grasses picked up the dried leaves and the odd scrap of paper and swirled them for a few seconds before setting them down again.

"Are you cold?" He let go of her hand, opened his jacket and wrapped it around her as he pulled her close. "We're almost there."

Oscar, happy to be with the two people he loved best, dropped a stick at Nat's feet and gave a joyful bark.

"Just one throw, you nutty dog. But don't you dare go into the water."

The dog happily chased the stick along the beach and arrived back with it just as they reached the Herrmann property. Nat took the stick before pushing the gate open, and Maggie and Oscar followed him to the back door where he bent to retrieve the key from under the coconut-fibre mat. It was gone.

"Perhaps the police used it to get into the house," Maggie said.

"But they had Adam's key. It was in his pocket, remember?"

Maggie nodded and reached past Nat for the door knob. A slight twist and the door opened. "Do you think there's someone in there?" she whispered.

Nat very quietly re-closed the door. "Let's have a look around the outside first," he whispered back. "Hang onto Oscar."

They walked all around the house, peering into windows. The place seemed quite deserted, and when they arrived back at their starting point, Nat said, "Wait here while I peek into the garage." He was back in a matter of minutes.

"The car's gone."

"Perhaps the police towed it away."

"Why would they do that?"

"It was a fairly new car—perhaps someone's pinched it. Damn! It's starting to rain again. Do you think we can slip inside until it eases up?"

Nat reopened the back door and then stopped. Maggie looked past his shoulder. "It's been cleaned up," she whispered, "and I don't think the cops were kind enough to do that. Quiet, Oscar," she added as he gave a little whimper.

Someone had definitely given the place a thorough cleaning. They could see right through into the living room, and the fruit and fruit flies were gone as were the beer bottles, the sticky peanut butter jar and the plate.

"I think," Nat whispered as he urged her out the door, "that we'd better leave."

But as Maggie hurried toward the back gate, she realized that Nat had detoured to the shed. "I'll just be a minute," he said.

"But suppose they come back?"

"Knock on the shed door, okay? And then head for the beach . . ."

Maggie, on tenterhooks, paced up and down outside the shed, while Oscar pressed his nose against the door, waiting for Nat to reappear from this place that had such interesting smells. But when weird scraping noises began inside the shed, the dog immediately sprang back and started to bark.

"Quiet, Oscar," Maggie whispered, scooping him up. Then in the sudden silence after he stopped barking, she heard a car's engine and realized it was the blue Buick re-entering the garage. Banging on the shed door, she shouted, "Nat! They're back!"

He poked his head out of the door and pointed urgently to the back gate. "Go!"

Not waiting to see if Nat was following, Maggie set Oscar on the ground and dragged him out of the gate and along the beach to where they'd left her car. Yanking open the door, she sank into the driver's seat with the excited dog on top of her. Moments later the passenger door opened and Nat, panting with the exertion, slid in beside her.

"That was a close call," he said, grinning.

"Too close for comfort. Let's get out of here." She started the car and, after checking in her rear view mirror, began backing toward the road then abruptly hit the brake as another car passed the end of the beach access lane. She waited another few moments before she began backing again then swung left to head up the hill.

"No," Nat said, "turn right."

"Right?" Maggie exclaimed.

"It's time we met Mr. and Mrs. Herrmann," Nat explained.

"I don't think so, Nat. If I'm not mistaken, that was Sergeant Allen in the police car that just passed behind us."

"What police car?"

"That one," she said, pointing a thumb over her shoulder at the car that was just coming to a stop in front of the Herrmanns' house.

Nat craned his neck to see it. "Do you think he saw us?"

"He didn't turn his head this way. . ."

"Well, let's wait and see what happens."

"We know what's going to happen, Nat. Allen is going to take them to identify their son. And if we wait around in that beach access, they're going to see my car as they pass. I'll give them a day or so then I'll call on them myself." She put the car into gear and started up the hill again. "So what was all that scraping I heard in the shed?"

"I wondered when you were going to ask. As I suspected, there was a trap door under the carpet, but it was locked and I couldn't find a key. I tried prying it up but it wouldn't budge."

"You really didn't expect them to leave a key nice and handy for you, did you?"

"Well, they left the key to the house under the back door mat. . ."

"That's true." Then, seeing a chance to get her own back, she added, "I hope you replaced the carpet just as you found it."

Knowing he had it coming, Nat said meekly, "Of course."

FIONA PLEADED A HEADACHE that evening so Nat was the only extra guest for dinner at the Rinaldis'. Afterwards, Bianca said, "I don't need help with clearing away, and I know you two have a lot to talk about."

"Thanks. We do have a lot to discuss before Nat heads back to the city in the morning," Maggie said, then knowing that her hosts were a bit old-fashioned, she asked, "Would you mind if Nat comes up to my room?"

Bianca laughed. "I think you two can be trusted."

The bedroom, although very pretty, had room for only a single bed, a dressing table, a night table and a cretonne-covered armchair set beside the window.

"Your choice," Maggie said. "Armchair or bed?"

"I'd like it to be the bed," he answered, gathering her into his arms, "but by the size of it, I can see your reputation is quite safe."

"It's surprising what one can do in a small space," she answered, lifting her face for another kiss.

MUCH LATER, PROPPED UP on pillows, they looked carefully at each page of Gordon's sketchbook. He had drawn St. Martin's Church from several angles, a group of children building a sandcastle on the beach, rowboats and canoes, apple trees laden with fruit, and two pages were covered with small, very rough sketches of gates and fences and doors.

Maggie was about to turn the page when Nat said, "Just a minute." He pointed. "I'm pretty sure that's the trap door in the shed in the back garden. I just wish I could have got it open and had a look." Then he had an awful thought and immediately turned to Maggie. "And don't you dare try to find out what's under that carpet yourself while I'm gone. Promise me, Maggie."

"Stop worrying. How could I get into the shed now that the Herrmanns have returned?"

"Knowing you, my gal, you could find a way."

But Maggie's thoughts were on another track entirely. "Nat, do you think Gordon killed Adam and then set the church on fire to hide his crime?"

Nat shook his head. "The chief says the fire was started from a cigarette butt in the wastepaper basket, and that's no way to start a fire if you want to burn down a church. Anyway, why would Gordon kill his friend?"

"Maybe it was an accident. Maybe they were horsing around and . . ."

"No, the wound that killed that boy was too cata-strophic to have been anything but deliberate."

"But what reason would anyone have to kill him? And who was the person in the cloak who was seen running away? That Jennings woman isn't very nice, but I don't think she was making that up. Do you think that could have been Gordon?"

"Where would he get a cloak? You said Schultz showed you *his* cloak . . ." Nat paused and then continued, "And even if Gordon was there when Adam was killed and that was him in the cloak, why didn't anyone remem-ber hearing his car driving away? Or was that the sound that woke Mrs. Jennings?"

"No, that would be in the wrong order. She said some-thing woke her and that's when she looked out the win-dow and saw the man in the cloak running away." Then she said, "But Nat, maybe he didn't drive away!" She picked up the sketch book again, flipped through the pages then pointed to a picture of a dark-haired person sitting at the oars of a rowboat. "Reverend Bicknell said they rowed over the first time, and maybe that's how they got there the night of the fire."

"But where's the boat now?" Nat said. "And if Gor-don was there when Adam was killed, he would have had to row back to Summerland to get his car—that is, if he was the one who crashed it at the junction . . ."

"And where is he now?"

They were both silent for a moment, then Nat said, "You know, Maggie, I'm beginning to wonder if this whole thing has more to do with the parents than the boys."

Maggie nodded in agreement. "I think you could be right."

"I'd better get going," he said, but he made no move to get up.

Maggie reached for her shoes. "Okay, I'll drive you back to your motel."

"Why don't you stay with me there?"

"I can't leave Oscar here on his own and, if you re-member, your motel has a 'no pets' policy."

They were on their way back to Penticton when Nat said, "You don't need to come and see me off in the morn-ing—my bus leaves very early."

"Don't worry, I'll be there." She reached over and patted his knee. "I'm going to miss you, you know. I just wish you were taking Fiona back with you."

Nat laughed. "Let's hope we find Gordon soon."

ALTHOUGH IT WAS AFTER midnight, they could see that Fiona's motel unit door was ajar, and as the car came to a stop, she didn't even wait for Nat to step out of it.

"I wondered where you'd got to," she said in an aggrieved voice. "Did you find out anything more about Gordon?

"No," Nat answered. "But the Herrmanns have come back, and Maggie will talk to them as soon as possible."

"But why didn't you talk to them today? They must know what's happened to Gordon."

"There was no opportunity to do that," Maggie, who had rolled down the driver's window, answered sharply. "The police took them to identify their son's body."

Fiona ignored her. "Then you can't go back to Vancouver tomorrow," Fiona told Nat. "You have to stay here and talk to those . . . those people. You have to find out what happened to my son."

"Fiona, I have other clients to see in Vancouver and meetings that have been arranged that can't be postponed. I promise that I will be back by the end of the week. In the meantime Maggie, who already knows more about this case than I do, will carry on here, and she will contact the Herrmanns as soon as she decently can."

"But I engaged *you* to find him."

"Maggie, as my partner, is just as capable. If you're not happy with this arrangement, you're free to engage someone else."

"You know that's not possible." She turned and gave Maggie a look of utter contempt. "I guess she'll have to do until you get back." And marching into her motel room, she slammed the door.

"Wow!" Maggie leaned out of her car window. "She doesn't like me very much, does she? Anyway, I'll see you about six-thirty in the morning."

He bent to kiss her tenderly, then smiling, he watched her drive out of the motel's courtyard.

THE NEXT MORNING AS PROMISED, Maggie and Oscar were back at the motel at six-thirty sharp. Nat was waiting with his weekend bag in hand.

"Thanks," he said as he fell into the passenger seat. "I'm bushed. Fiona came to my room and insisted on going over and over and over everything that's happened."

Trying not to laugh, Maggie said gently, "Perhaps you should choose your female clients a bit more carefully."

"WELL, OSCAR," MAGGIE SAID fifteen minutes later as they watched the bus disappear around the bend, "it's just you and me again. Except for that dratted woman," she finished under her breath.

CHAPTER FOURTEEN

"You look absolutely bushed." George Sawasky, a cup of coffee in each hand, peered around the door into Nat's office.

"You'd be bushed too if you'd sat on that damned bus for six hours. Did you know it stops at every tiny village and crossroads along the way? Thought we'd never get to Vancouver. Thanks," he added as George placed the steaming cup before him. "How did things go here?"

"Not too bad." He kicked the office door closed. "I know we laugh about Henny and her cookies, but she really is a godsend when it comes to digging up information or the right files."

Nat grinned. "Maggie's trained her well—though sometimes almost too well as she thinks she's a better detective than either of us and insists on giving us—and sometimes our clients—good advice."

"I must admit she tried that on me, but I let it go." George pulled up a chair across from his boss. "I don't suppose you've had time to look at the files I left out for you."

"I've had a quick glance. Doesn't look like you had any problems. . ."

George shook his head. "If you remember, they were mostly follow-ups."

"Great. Did you manage to interview Wilhelm Herrmann?"

"I called the factory several times, but his secretary claimed he was either too busy or out. I eventually got us an interview for this afternoon at two. Hope that's okay?"

Nat nodded. "Wonder why he was so reluctant to talk to you?" he mused. "Anyway, bring me up to date on these," he added, drawing the files toward him.

HERRMANN BROTHERS TENT AND AWNING was a three-storey, square yellow building in the east end of the city. Luckily, as the street was jammed with traffic, there was a parking lot at the back. As Nat and George climbed out of the car, a truck pulled up to a large receiving dock, the door opened and a couple of hefty men with a forklift immediately began unloading huge bales of coloured canvas.

There didn't seem to be an entrance at the back of the building other than the dock, so Nat led the way around to the front. Somewhere within the bowels of the building machines hummed and roared, but the reception area, manned by a prim, grey-haired woman, was quiet, dusty and unwelcoming.

"Yes?" she asked, glaring at them over her half-moon glasses.

"Southby and Sawasky to see Mr. Herrmann."

She glanced down at a large reception book and solemnly ticked them off. "Take a seat." She indicated two spindly cane chairs set against the wall. "I'll let him know you're here," she said, picking up the phone. It was at least ten minutes before the only other door in the reception area opened and a girl who couldn't have been much more than fifteen appeared.

"I'm to take you up to Mr. Herrmann's office," she explained in a voice not much above a whisper.

As they followed her up three flights of concrete stairs, the noise of machinery grew louder and louder. Nat was out of puff and literally hanging onto the iron hand railing by the time she opened the door on the third floor landing where the noise suddenly swelled to a crescendo. In front of them were massive machines to cut the canvas, machines to insert grommets, and rows and rows of power sewing machines operated by women of all ages, but Nat noticed that a good many of them were youngsters no older than the girl leading them toward a row of glass-enclosed offices.

"This is Mr. Herrmann's office," the girl said, knocking timidly. She opened the door but before Nat could thank her, she had turned and fled toward the machines.

Nat had somehow been expecting a large, blustery man to go with all the noisy machines, but instead Wilhelm Herrmann was of medium height and so lean that his clothes hung on him. He indicated two chairs in front of his scarred desk.

"What can I do for you gentlemen?"

"You know about the death of your nephew Adam?"

Wilhelm Herrmann nodded. "I understand he was in a church when it burned down, but what he was doing in a church I can't begin to guess. You. . ." he looked down at Nat's card, "are private detectives. Did my brother engage you?"

"No. We are looking into the disappearance of Adam's friend, Gordon Phelps. He was in the Okanagan on holiday with Adam and he went missing around the same time that Adam was killed."

"I don't understand. How can I help you with this boy's disappearance? After all, my nephew's death was in Naramata and I'm here in Vancouver."

"The two boys were supposed to be coming back to Vancouver together," George said, leaning towards Herrmann's desk, "and we understand that Adam was expected back here just after Labour Day to begin working for you. Weren't you surprised when he didn't turn up?"

Wilhelm Herrmann shook his head. "Why would I be surprised? Young people today are all unreliable. No," he said, shaking his head again. "No, I wasn't a bit surprised. I blame my brother for not being stricter with him. If he had been, the boy would still be alive. Is there anything else I can help you with?"

"Your brother Peter is a partner in this tent and awning business, too, isn't he?"

"Peter? Yes, of course he is. He does the selling and buying. He travels a lot getting orders, selling our products and getting us good prices for the stock we use. He has a head for that kind of thing."

"So where was he when his son was murdered?" Nat asked.

"Murdered! What do you mean—murdered? The police told me he was found dead in a burned-out church."

"He was hit over the head with an iron bar," Nat said. "So where were his parents?"

A look of fear crossed the man's face, but he quickly pulled himself together. "In Calgary. Rosa's mother had a heart attack and they rushed there to see her. She died a few days after they got there." Still visibly shaken, Herrmann got to his feet and walked around the desk. "Is there anything else?"

"Yes," George answered. "Have you any idea what young Adam was into? Why would such a young kid be so viciously killed?"

A look of fury came over Wilhelm's face and he took a threatening step toward George. "What are you suggesting?" He poked George in the chest. "That someone in my family was up to no good? Perhaps you should be taking a closer look at this other boy. . . this Gordon or whatever his name is. Seems suspicious to me that my nephew gets killed and this other boy conveniently disappears."

"Cool down." Nat quickly put himself between the two men. "Mr. Herrmann, you can rest assured that we, as well as the police, are looking at all the angles."

"The police said they'd pinned the fire on some weird organist."

"No. They've ruled the organist out as a suspect," Nat answered quietly. He walked toward the door and extended his hand, but it was totally ignored as Herrmann opened the door and waited for them to leave.

"I take it you can find your own way down the stairs?" Herrmann said before closing the door firmly behind them. But they remained outside the door listening, and just as they expected, less than a minute later they heard him yelling into the phone: "So what the hell went wrong?"

BACK IN THE CAR Nat sat for a moment, tapping his fingers on the steering wheel. "You know what, George? I think it's time we spoke to the grandparents."

"Grandparents? You mean Fiona's mum and dad?"

Nat nodded as he started the engine and set off across town. "And there's no time like the present."

"Shouldn't you call first? She did say that they are elderly and not too healthy."

"We'll wait until we see them, then play it by ear."

"You have their address?"

"Same as Fiona's. They live on West 13th near Alma Road.

NAT LED THE WAY through the small, well-kept garden to the front door of the two-storey house and rang the bell.

"You've been here before?" George asked as they waited.

"Yeah. Fiona insisted on us taking her car to the Okanagan, so I had to take a cab here." Nat pressed the doorbell again.

"I'm coming," a voice called out and a moment later the door was opened by a woman who was probably in her late seventies. One could easily see that she was related to Fiona as she was tall and upright and had the same green eyes and thin mouth.

"Yes?"

"I'm Nat Southby and this is my associate George Sawasky," Nat said, extending his business card.

She looked down at the card with a puzzled expression. "It says you're a private investigator. I don't understand."

"Fiona, your daughter, hired us to look into the disappearance of your grandson, Gordon," Nat explained.

"What do you mean—Gordon's disappearance? Gordon hasn't disappeared. He's on vacation."

"Look, Mrs. Phelps, could we come in? We need to ask you a few questions."

"What is it, dear?"

Mrs. Phelps turned to the man who had suddenly appeared behind her. "It's about our Gordon. This man says he's disappeared. They want to come in and ask us some questions."

"Disappeared? Nonsense. He's with that friend of his . . .what was his name. . ?

"Adam Herrmann," she supplied. "Nice young man."

"That's right. If you're looking for Gordon, you'd better ask. . .what was his name again, Florence?"

"Adam. He went to school with Gordon." She turned back to Nat and George. "Fiona has gone to bring Gordon back from the Okanagan. His car broke down, you see. I don't know where you got the idea he's disappeared."

"Does Gordon's father keep in touch with him?" George asked.

"Gordon didn't have a father. We're all the parents he needed. I don't know who hired you," she added, giving Nat's card back to him, "but it certainly wasn't Fiona."

The two men were suddenly faced with another closed door.

"It obvious that our Miss Phelps still hasn't told them about their grandson," George said, leading the way back to the car. "I wonder if Maggie has found out anything more?" he added as he climbed into the passenger seat.

"She always calls me around six-thirty. I'll know then."

"When are you returning to Naramata?"

"I'm not sure. It's not fair my leaving you to cope on your own."

"I can see your quandary, Nat," George answered slowly. "I only signed up for part-time work, but this is a special situation. As long as you feel you can trust my judgement, I'm willing to hold the fort here while you go back to Penticton."

"What's Lucille going to say about it? After all, you're supposed to be retired."

"Lucille will be delighted."

"Delighted? But she's been looking forward to your retirement for years."

"She's already fed up with me trying to organize her work routine, hates me going shopping with her, and keeps telling me to find a nice hobby."

Nat laughed. "Well, if you're really sure, I'll let Maggie know that I'll be back there by the end of the week. That will give us time to go over our other cases and decide the best way to tackle them. And Henny will be thrilled to bits to have you to fuss over."

"Blast! I forgot about her damn cookies." George climbed out of the car and headed for the building's entrance.

"It's your own fault. You kept telling her how much you love them." Nat was still laughing as they climbed the stairs.

CHAPTER FIFTEEN

The door was opened by a dark-haired woman, her eyes red and swollen from crying. "If you're selling something. . ."

It was mid-morning on Monday, and though Maggie would have preferred to wait another day before going to see the Herrmanns, Fiona had been determined they would go that day. Still, Maggie had managed to stall so that it was ten o'clock before they left for Summerland.

Now she extended her card to the bereaved woman. "Mrs. Herrmann, I'm Maggie Spencer and this is our agency's client, Miss Fiona Phelps."

Rosa Herrmann looked up from the card. "Is this about Adam? But he's dead! My boy is dead. Go away!"

"Yes, I know and I am so sorry, but we are trying to locate Adam's friend, Gordon Phelps. He was staying here with you."

"Gordon . . ?"

"What's going on, Rosa?" A thick-set man dressed in a three-piece tweed suit suddenly appeared behind his wife. "What do you want?" He glared at Maggie and Fiona. "Why have you upset my wife?"

"Her card says she's a detective." Rosa Herrmann passed it over to him. "She says it's about that friend of Adam's who was staying here . . ."

"He's missing," Fiona burst out. "My son Gordon is missing! Where is he? Have you murdered him, too?"

Maggie put a hand on Fiona's arm in an effort to calm her, but Fiona brushed it off.

"What have you done with my son?" she yelled.

Peter Herrmann suddenly looked frightened. "But I sent Gordon back to Vancouver. Are you telling me he didn't get there?"

Rosa tugged on her husband's arm. "You said Adam had gone back to Vancouver with him."

Shrugging her off, he said, "Rosa's mother had a heart attack so we had to go to Calgary. I told Gordon to go back to Vancouver, but Adam had to stay behind here to do a job for me. He was coming into the business with Wilhelm and me."

"What job?" Rosa grabbed at her husband's arm again. "What did you make him do?"

Peter Herrmann pushed his wife into the house. "Come on, get inside. We've answered enough questions."

Though uninvited, Maggie and Fiona followed.

"So you've been in Calgary all this time," Maggie insisted, "and that's why the police and my agency couldn't locate you."

"My mother died." Rosa sank into a chair and buried her face in her hands. "First my mother and now my son. . .my baby boy . . .how. . .how. . .am I going to bear it?" And she began sobbing uncontrollably.

"What was the job your son was doing for you?" Maggie asked.

"That`s none of your business!"

"But that job got him killed."

"Now don't you blame his death on me! If young Gordon's missing. . ." He raised his hands. "Maybe he's the reason Adam got killed . . ."

Rosa suddenly turned on her husband. "That's why those men were so angry, wasn't it? That's why they came in here shouting at you!"

"Shut the hell up, Rosa. That was all a misunderstan—"

"No, no. It was more than that. They were nasty, violent men. Oh, dear God! What if they come back?"

"They won't if they know what`s good for them." And he began trying to herd Maggie and Fiona out the door. "Get out of my house! We've told you all we're going to tell you . . ."

But Maggie stood her ground. "Reverend Bicknell saw both of the boys outside St. Martin's church a few days before the fire. And he said they had rowed across the lake. I take it you own a rowboat?"

Rosa Herrmann was now standing behind her husband wailing in grief.

"No, I don't own a rowboat!" And he started pushing Maggie and Fiona out the door. "Get out! Get out!" Then just before he shut the door, he yelled, "What about Gordon's car? You find that car and you'll find the guy who murdered my son!"

Maggie stuck her foot in the door to prevent him fully closing it. "The police already found the car. It was abandoned on a side road near Kaleden Point, all smashed up."

"Well, that answers your question, doesn't it?" he shouted from behind the door. "He killed Adam then ran away!"

"Gordon didn't murder your son!" Fiona screamed at him. "Your son is responsible for Gordon being missing—"

Maggie pushed the door wide open again. "I've written both the address where I'm staying and Miss Phelps motel on the back of my card. Call me if you hear anything more." She took Fiona's arm and started up the path as the door slammed behind them.

"No!" Fiona said, pulling away. "I'm going back in there and make that man tell us what happened to Gordon!"

Maggie kept walking toward the car. "He's not going to tell us, Fiona. Maybe when he thinks it over, he might have some more information for us, but he's not going to tell us anything more right now." She got into the car and waited, and after a few minutes Fiona reluctantly followed. She was crying bitterly as she climbed into the car.

"You know, if Adam was going into the family business," Maggie said as they drove away, "Wilhelm Herrmann must've wondered why the boy didn't report for work. I must ask Nat if he's talked to him."

"I don't care about all that stuff," Fiona howled. "I just want to find Gordon, and what are you and your so-called boss doing about that?"

"Whatever it takes," Maggie answered quietly. She would not allow herself to be pushed into saying something she would regret. "I'll drop you off at your motel," she said as they approached Penticton.

"No," Fiona snapped. "Take me to this place where Gordon"s car crashed. And then I want to speak to that stupid Sergeant Allen again. Maybe he's found out something you and your so-called detective agency haven't been able to find out."

Low black clouds had once more gathered to hide the watery sun by the time the two women arrived at Kaleden Junction. Raindrops started to splatter on the windshield as they drove down the side road and stopped to gaze silently at the huge scrape on the trunk of one of the jack pines—the only visual sign that Gordon's car had ever been there.

"Seen enough?" Maggie asked.

Fiona nodded. "Let's go back."

"I thought you wanted to see Sergeant Allen."

"What's the use?" Fiona answered forlornly. "He doesn't know anything."

It was with a distinct feeling of relief that Maggie drew up outside Fiona's motel unit.

"I'll call you as soon as I hear anything," she said and waited until Fiona had found her key in her handbag and inserted it in the lock before she put the car into gear. She was looking over her shoulder with the car in reverse when she realized that Fiona was frantically banging on the passenger side window. She hit the brake and reached over to roll down the window. "What's the matter?"

"This!" Fiona screamed at her, waving a piece of paper. "It's a note from Gordon!"

Maggie quickly pulled forward again, turned off the engine and flung the door open.

"It was pushed under the door!" Fiona was shaking from head to foot as she thrust the piece of paper into Maggie's hands. It says . . . here, you read it."

Taking the note from Fiona's hands, Maggie read it out aloud.

Sis. They say I took their money and they are going to kill me if you don't come up with $100,000. They will telephone and tell you where the drop-off will be and, whatever you do, don't call the police.

"Where would I get $100,000?" Fiona was howling again, and Maggie led her into the motel unit, sat her down on the bed and closed the door. Then she strode to the telephone, and after securing an outside line, she phoned Nat's office.

"Nat. Get back here as soon as you can," she ordered when he picked up the phone. "We've got a note from Gordon. Listen. . ." And she read the note to him.

CHAPTER SIXTEEN

Maggie awoke with a start and lay on her back while she tried to pull herself together. It was daylight and to prove it a pallid sun was shining through the window. Turning on her side she peered at her alarm clock.

"Good grief! Nine-thirty!" Sitting up, she swung her legs over the side of the bed. *It's so quiet. Why hadn't the dog wakened her?*

"Where are you, Oscar?"

But his basket was empty and there was a cold cup of coffee on the little table beside her bed. She had been so bushed the night before—mentally as well as physically. Fiona was a difficult client to deal with at the best of times, but the ransom note had sent her way over the top. It had taken Maggie a good couple of hours to calm her enough that she was in a fit state to leave her alone—and this was only after she received multiple promises that Maggie would follow the note's instruction and not call the police.

"But," she muttered as she slipped into the bathroom, "I'm damn well going to call Sergeant Allen as soon as I'm dressed." She was in the act of pulling on her slacks when Bianca knocked on the door and then burst into the bedroom.

"Maggie! You've got to see this." And she thrust the *Penticton Herald* at her. "See, see this article."

Maggie took the paper from her and sat down on the side of the bed to read the front page story:

Samuel Bennet, eleven, and his nine-year-old brother, Harry, caused a minor sensation yesterday when they found an abandoned rowboat which had drifted ashore. Mrs. Bennet, the boys' mother, was immediately concerned when they produced a priest's cassock with Reverend Bicknell's name sewn inside. Fearing that the popular clergyman had accidently drowned, she immediately phoned the police. The Penticton Herald is happy to report that the Reverend is safe, but the police have taken the boat into custody because of its peculiar cargo. The police are not revealing what that cargo is, but Mrs. Bennet told our reporter that there were about 20 oil-skin-wrapped packages in the boat. Our reporter has also interviewed the Reverend but he knew nothing about the boat or its contents and had no knowledge how his cassock could possibly have been in the boat.

"Oil-skin-wrapped packages!" Maggie exclaimed. "That sounds exactly like drugs to me. But surely those boys couldn't have been dealing drugs. . ."

"The Bennet boys?"

"No, no. Fiona's son and his friend."

Bianca shook her head in dismay. "No, no. It is impossible. They are not much older than my Lorenzo and Bellissa."

"I must telephone the sergeant right away." Maggie slipped on her shoes and reached for her handbag.

"I have made you some scrambled eggs," Bianca said as she trailed Maggie down to the kitchen. "You must eat first."

"Thank you, Bianca. Please keep them warm for me."

"It's about that boat those two kids found," she told Allen when she eventually got through to him. "And Fiona has heard from her son, Gordon."

"She's found him?"

"No. She's received a ransom note. Look, I'm on my way to see you and I'll fill you in on the details then."

MAGGIE SPREAD THE NEWSPAPER on Allen's desk. "The boat these kids found has to be the one Gordon and Adam used to row across the lake to Naramata," she told him. "I don't know what the cassock was doing in the boat, but it sure links Gordon's abduction and Adam's murder in the church. I surmise the oil-skin bags contain drugs of some kind—but I find it very hard to believe those boys were mixed up in this."

"And you say she got a ransom note?"

"Last night."

"Why the hell didn't she call me right away?"

"Because it specifies she's not to call the police, and she's absolutely terrified that Gordon will be murdered like Adam."

"You'd better be with me when I confront her," Allen said, grabbing his coat. "Come on."

"She's going to be furious with me," Maggie said as she tried to keep up with his long strides to an unmarked police car. "And she'll blame me if anything happens to that boy."

He turned to her before he slipped behind the wheel of the car. "Listen to me. You've done the right thing."

"I hope I *have* done the right thing," Maggie muttered as she prepared to follow him in her own vehicle. "Suppose they find out that I've told the police and they do kill him?"

"I told you *no police*," Fiona screamed when the sergeant and Maggie entered her motel room.

"Just show me the letter," Allen demanded.

Tears streaming down her face, Fiona reluctantly passed it over. "Gordon expressly says no police. It will be *your* fault," she whimpered, pointing at Maggie, "if they kill him."

"You're sure this is his handwriting?" Allen asked her.

She nodded.

"Has he ever been mixed up with drugs?"

"Gordon? Of course he hasn't. He doesn't even smoke."

"But he knew Adam Herrmann in Vancouver, and it's obvious the Herrmann boy was mixed up in the drug trade. And he knew him well enough to accept an invitation to go to his parents' place in Summerland."

"They went to the same high school, that's all, Sergeant. And Adam was his lab partner. Gordon just wanted time away before starting university."

"I'll take this with me," he said as he placed the letter into an evidence bag. "And I'll need you both to come to the station and have your prints taken before I can check for others on this letter. Have you anything belonging to your son?"

Fiona shook her head. "I don't think so."

"What about his sketch book?" Maggie suggested. "I still have it in my car."

"Depends how many others have handled it. . ."

"As far as I know just Gordon, Maggie and myself," Fiona answered.

"And my partner, Nat," Maggie said.

"Okay. Get it for me and you both get to the station ASAP."

Fiona waited until Allen had left before she swung around to confront Maggie. "How could you call him when I expressly told you not to?" she shouted.

"You'd better read this." Maggie spread the newspaper on the bed.

"What is it?"

"Just read it, Fiona."

"Oh, my God," Fiona cried after reading the article. "So that's why the sergeant asked if Gordon was mixed up with drugs! But I swear he wasn't. He didn't even smoke." Picking up the paper, she sat down hard on the side of the bed to read the article once more. "But how did the minister's cassock get into the boat?"

"I don't know. But after I've been to the station to give them my finger prints, I intend to find out. Are you coming with me?"

"I have to stay here in case they call again."

"If they do," Maggie said earnestly, "stall them and please don't do anything stupid like agreeing to hand over money."

"Even if it means saving my son's life?"

"Tell them all your money is in Vancouver and it will take days for you to get that much money transferred."

CHAPTER SEVENTEEN

After Maggie had her fingerprints taken, she headed across the road to the phone box she had used before. Once through to the office of Southby and Spencer Investigations, she had to cut Henny's chatter short and insist on being put straight through to Nat.

"But how in heaven's name did the Reverend's cassock get into the boat?" Nat asked after she'd read the newspaper article to him.

"I've no idea," Maggie said, "but I intend to find out. Remember I told you he has two parishes to look after, and he was definitely in Kelowna when the fire broke out. So I don't think there's any way he could have been in that rowboat. But his cassock definitely ties the boat and its contents to the church."

"And the stuff in those oil-skin bags has to be the reason Adam Herrmann was in the church," Nat said.

"But what about Gordon Phelps? After all, he's missing, though it's hard to believe that he would have been mixed up in this kind of racket. After all, the family lives in Dunbar. . ."

Nat laughed. "You are *so* innocent, Maggie! When I was on the force, I saw a lot meaner kids coming from good families than the kids from the wrong side of town."

"Innocent?"

"Okay, I take that back."

"I should hope. Nat, there is no way whatever that Fiona Phelps would have allowed her son to be mixed up in anything criminal. She hovered over him like a mother hen! This was the first time she had even let him to go anywhere with the Herrmann kid."

"So you're saying that Adam Herrmann was running a drug racket all by himself?"

"No," Maggie answered, "I've been mulling this over, Nat. What if it's the father?"

"Okay, I'm with you there. If he's anything like his brother, he's probably up to his ears in it. Wilhelm Herrmann is one sleazy character!"

"And when Fiona and I went to see Peter Herrmann, he tried to throw us out as soon as we started asking questions . . ."

"So what if Gordon was with this Herrmann kid at the church?"

"And somehow he got away. . ."

"In the rowboat. . ."

"And that's why the Reverend's cassock was in the boat."

"I don't follow you, Maggie . . ."

"What if Georgina Jennings really did see somebody in a cloak running away? What if Gordon had grabbed the Reverend's cassock to disguise himself and she mistook him for Mr. Schultz."

"But. . . ."

"And," Maggie continued before Nat could disagree, "Gordon managed to escape in the rowboat that he and Adam had used to cross the lake—and he left the cassock behind in it."

"But how did the cocaine get into the boat?"

"You mean those oil-skin packets?"

There was silence on the line for a moment, and then Nat said, "What if we've got this backwards? What if it was the killers who escaped in the boat with the cocaine?"

"So what was the cassock doing in the boat?"

"I haven't figured that out," Nat said.

"But why would they kidnap Gordon and steal his car and then demand $100,000 to get him back if they had the cocaine?"

There was another silence while they considered this.

Suddenly Nat shouted, "That's the reason they kidnapped Gordon! They *didn't* get the money for the consignment of drugs, so they're demanding $100,000 from Fiona to make up for it!"

"But if Adam was buying drugs from them, surely he would have come there with the money to pay them. . ."

"But if he didn't bring the money," Nat said, "it could still be back there at the Herrmanns' house."

"But we searched the house."

"So where else could it be?"

"The shed!" they yelled at the same time.

"Under the trapdoor!" Nat added.

"I think you're right, Nat! The church was the rendezvous point and the kid didn't bring the money."

"We'll go and see the Herrmanns as soon as I get there tomorrow morning and get to the bottom of this."

When he got off the phone, Nat headed for George's office. "I'm leaving now. I have to make arrangements for the girl next door to look after Maggie's cat and pack a bag. I promised Maggie I'd be there by morning." He turned to Henny, "Look after George, okay?" And he marched out the door, snagging his raincoat off the wicker stand as he went by.

"NO," GEORGINA JENNINGS SAID adamantly, "it was that Karl Schultz I saw running down the street. And he was wearing that stupid cloak. I saw him with my own eyes."

Maggie stood her ground on the Jennings front porch. "But," she asked, "could it have possibly been someone wearing Reverend Bicknell's cassock? After all, it was one o'clock in the morning. . ."

"Don't be stupid! Why would anyone be wearing the Reverend's cassock? I know what I saw. It was that German." And once again Maggie was faced with a shut door.

When she went looking for Anthony Bicknell, his housekeeper told her that he had meetings all afternoon but would be home in the evening. She suggested that Maggie come back around seven.

"Okay, Oscar, you're one lucky dog," Maggie told him when she returned to the Apple Orchard B&B. "We've got time for a run along the beach." Oscar was only too happy. He'd been cooped up in Bianca's kitchen most of the day while Maggie had been dealing with Fiona and looking for the Reverend.

IT WAS NEARLY FIVE O'CLOCK and Henny was preparing to leave for the day when George Sawasky emerged from his office and stood before her desk. "Come into my office please, Henny," he said.

"Yes, Mr. George. Do I need my notebook?"

"No."

As she followed him to his office, she asked, "Are we doing detecting, Mr. George?"

He nodded. "Indeed we are, Henny, indeed we are. That is, if you can do a little overtime work tonight."

Henny reached for the phone. "I will call Hans, my husband. He will look after our boys until I get home." After the short conversation with her husband ended, she turned back to George. "Now what do I do?"

"You'll have to wear a disguise for this job." He reached under his desk and brought out a large paper bag and a turquoise hat with a broad, floppy brim. He dumped the contents of the bag onto his desk—a long, flowered turquoise silk scarf, a flowing white jacket and white gloves. "This is it."

"You want me to put them on, Mr. George?"

"Yep."

A few minutes later Henny stood before him in all her new finery. The hat was just right, but the white jacket that had reached nearly to Lucille's knees came just past Henny's hips. However, it would have to do. He adjusted the hat and scarf until he was satisfied that they produced the right effect, but he sighed as he looked down at her brogues. Unfortunately Lucille didn't own any shoes Henny's size.

"All right," he said as he adjusted the scarf around her neck one last time. "We're off. I'll explain what you have to do on the way." As they headed out the door, he suddenly stopped in his tracks. "Do you smoke, Henny?"

"No, *never*, Mr. George."

He shrugged. "I'll give you a lesson on the way to our stake-out."

Henny gave an anxious smile. "You mean I really haf to smoke?"

"You can pretend."

She gave a satisfied smile as she followed him down the stairs. She was going to have a stake-out of her very own!

"Now, Henny, have you got it straight?" George asked anxiously as he drove into the first available parking spot behind the hotel.

Henny nodded. "I go into the cocktail lounge and I sit on a high stool at the bar and I order a drink." She paused for a moment. "But Mr. George, I don't drink."

"Oh! Well, just order a soda with a twist of lemon, okay?"

"Yes. Soda with a twist of lemon. Then I pretend to smoke? "

George gave an inward shudder at the thought of his accomplice juggling a glass of soda and trying to light a cigarette. "No. Forget the cigarette. Just sip the soda and keep an eye on the lobby for our quarry."

"And when he arrives, I follow up in the elevator."

"But you must be very careful because he might recognize you. . ."

"He only sees me once, Mr. George, and now I wear my disguise," she said, readjusting her hat for the tenth time.

"But Henny, you are very. . . uh. . .distinctive." *And that's putting it mildly,* he thought. "He could possibly recognize you if he sees you up close."

"I will be very careful. Then I see what door he goes in and I try to see who is with him."

"Perhaps this isn't such a good idea."

"No, no. I will be all right. You see."

George watched with trepidation as she marched into the hotel, and his trepidation turned into absolute fear when ten minutes later the dark blue Chrysler pulled up a few spaces away from him.

There were only a few people seated at the bar when Henny climbed up onto a stool and ordered her soda with a twist of lemon. She was just a couple of seats from a very smartly dressed woman, and Henny looked covertly at the high heels, nylon stockings and very expensive fur wrap, envying them, but as Mr. George had instructed, she sipped her drink, all the time keeping an eye on the nearby lobby entrance as if she was waiting for a friend to join her. She felt very important and thought how Mr. Nat would be so proud of her doing a real sleuthing job. But

she almost fell off her stool in surprise when the mark—
she had seen that word in the detective stories she read—
walked right up to the lady in the fur wrap and slipped his
arm around her shoulders.

"Waiting long?"

Henny quickly bent her head so that the floppy brim
of her hat covered her face and began gulping her drink.
Unfortunately, the bubbles got up her nose and she had to
stifle the sneeze that threatened to blow the whole operation. But she needn't have worried because the two were
so engrossed in each other that they had no eyes for
Henny. She watched from beneath her hat brim as the
woman slid off her stool and the two of them walked toward the elevators.

It took her a few minutes to remember that she was
supposed to follow them. Slamming her glass down on
the bar, she almost fell off the stool in her haste to get over
to the elevators, but the elegant door slid shut in her face,
and she watched in dismay as the pointer slowly marked
its ascent. It eventually stopped at the fourth floor. For a
moment she thought about running out to the car park and
telling Mr. George that his suspicions were correct, but he
had given her explicit orders to follow them up. Un-
daunted, she hopped into the next elevator, punched the
button for four and willed it to go fast. When the door
opened on the fourth floor, she stepped out into the corridor. There was no sign of the two she was supposed to
follow—in fact, the corridor was empty—and she was

about to hit the button to go down again when she heard a man speaking.

"Make yourself comfortable while I get some ice."

She was sure it was the quarry that Mr. George had told her to follow, but he would have to pass her to get to the ice machine. She was trapped, and as she was the only person in the entire hallway, he was bound to recognize her. Making sure her floppy hat was well over her face, she walked over to stand in front of the nearest door and delved into her oversized bag, pretending to look for her key. It seemed an eternity before she heard him approach. For a moment his footsteps faltered as if he was going to speak to her, but to her relief he carried on.

Henny waited until she was sure he had turned the corner before she loped down the passageway to see what his room number was. 436. She would have to remember that to tell Mr. George. "436, 436, 436 . . ." she muttered to herself as she raced toward the exit sign and clattered down the four flights of stairs.

George was beside himself with worry. Twice he had climbed out of his car and started for the hotel, but each time he realized that he had to put his faith in his partner-in-criminal investigation. But it was taking a lot of faith. Glancing at his watch for the umpteenth time, he was about to go and find her when he saw her running toward him, the floppy hat in one hand and her enormous bag gripped in the other.

"436!" Henny cried as she flung herself into the passenger seat.

George sighed with relief.

FIONA OPENED HER MOTEL room door and glared at Maggie. "Where have you been all day? I've been here all alone worrying myself to death over my son."

"Have you heard from the kidnappers again?"

Fiona thrust a piece of paper at Maggie. "They left this at the motel office. It's from Gordon."

"That means he's still alive."

"No thanks to you."

Maggie didn't respond but instead read Gordon's note aloud:

Sis, you have twenty-four hours to get the $100,000 or they'll kill me. I will send a note to you tomorrow to tell you where to make the drop. Please don't call the police.

"Have you told them?"

"With Gordon's life hanging in the balance? Of course not!"

"Fiona, the police have got to know. Put your coat on. We're taking it to them right away." And Maggie headed for her car.

Reluctantly Fiona followed.

"WHY DIDN'T YOU CALL me as soon as you got it?" Sergeant Allen asked as he placed the note on his desk. "If we hope to get your son back safely, we have to know what those thugs are planning."

"But I'm trying to protect him!" Fiona answered as the tears streamed down her face. "He says they'll kill him if I go to the police. Put yourself in my place."

"I do understand," Sergeant Allen said, "but you must realize these people will just go on asking for more and more. If they get in touch with you again, please, please call me immediately."

Once Maggie had returned Fiona to the motel, promising that Nat would be there by morning, she drove thoughtfully back toward the B&B. She wondered how she and Nat would tackle the Herrmanns the following morning. *It's got to be the father who's mixed up in the drug scene. That boy was far too young to be a drug dealer. . .* At that moment she realized that two cars ahead of her was a wood-panelled station wagon. After a couple of miles it turned off into an orchard, but it wasn't until she came abreast of its turn-off that she realized it was the same place where she had nearly been side-swiped. *That's the same bloody car!*

PROMPTLY AT SEVEN THAT evening, Maggie and Oscar were back at Anthony Bicknell's house, and as promised he was in. "Do you have any idea how or why anyone could have stolen your cassock?" she asked as he poured coffee.

"Absolutely no idea. But you know it would be very easy to do. I keep one in the vestry of each church—St. Mary's in Kelowna and one here in St. Martin's. So it could have been stolen any time between Wednesday when I left here and Saturday night when the church burned down. So it doesn't necessarily have anything to do with the fire and that boy being killed here."

Maggie shook her head. "I'm sure Gordon Phelps took it from your vestry that night because Georgina Jennings saw a man in a cape running away from the fire. She was sure it was Karl Schultz because he owns a cape, but we've already proved it wasn't him."

"So have you found the Phelps boy?"

"No. That's the problem we're facing now. He's been kidnapped and they're holding him for a ransom of $100,000. His mother has no way of raising that kind of money."

"My goodness! This is terrible. That kind of thing doesn't happen here in Naramata. Why would they do such a thing?"

"Drugs. That's what police found in that rowboat— along with your cassock."

Anthony Bicknell looked stricken. "Are you sure? I can't see those nice boys being mixed up with drugs."

"I can't either. Besides, a couple of kids could never deal in drugs on this scale. But my partner and I have a hunch that all this has to do with Adam Herrmann's father."

"But the police are involved now so they'll get to the bottom of it."

"I'm not so sure about that. I don't think they are asking that man the right questions." As she stood up to leave, she added, "I've a good mind to go and talk to him myself."

"Perhaps you should leave that to the police, Mrs. Spencer," Bicknell said, but Maggie was already out the door.

Instead of turning off at the B&B, Maggie continued on the road south, determined to investigate the orchard where she had seen the station wagon turn in. "It's all right, Oscar," she assured the dog as she neared the orchard. "We'll just take a little peek. There's no need for Nat to know."

Fortunately, as they approached the turn-off to the orchard, the wood-panelled station wagon erupted onto the road and headed for Penticton. "See, Oscar? Everything is going to be fine—they've gone."

She turned into the driveway, and her little red car began bouncing down the narrow gravel track between the apple trees. A slight wind was loosening the first leaves of autumn, and they drifted down over the car as she passed a narrow lane that branched off to her left and she glimpsed a big house among the trees, but she continued on between the fruit trees to the farthest edge of the property where the track suddenly turned to the right. *So where in heaven's name did that station wagon come from?* She was just about to conclude it had come from the big house when just beyond the last row of apple trees she saw a row of shuttered cabins. *Pickers' cabins!* Pulling up in front of the first one, she stopped the car and got out. "You stay there, Oscar. I'll be right back."

The first cabin was unlocked but empty as was the second one, but she struck gold on the third. Liquor bottles and empty cans were piled by the door and the weeds beside it had been flattened where a car had been recently parked. This time the door was locked. She stepped around the corner to the single window, shaded her eyes with her hands and peered into the dark interior. Then as she turned to go back to her car, her attention was caught by a slight movement inside the room. Quickly she ran back to the car, opened the door and flung herself into the driver's seat. "Let's get the hell out of here, Oscar!" Her hand was on the ignition key when she stopped. "But why didn't he come after me?" Cautiously she opened the car door again and stepped out.

Back at the cabin window she caught the movement again inside. This time she tapped on the glass and called out, "Gordon? Gordon, is that you? It's okay, I'll get you out of there!" She ran around to the door and rattled the handle then threw herself at the door, shoulder first. It may have worked wonders in the movies she had seen, but it had no effect on this one. She ran to her car, opened the trunk and grabbed the tire wrench. Back at the cabin she inserted the wrench close to the door handle and heaved on it. It took several tries before it popped open.

"Gordon?"

A red-haired boy was huddled on a bunk at the far end of the single room, tied hand and foot to the bed post, a filthy gag in his mouth. She ran over to him and ripped the gag off. "Gordon?"

"Yes," he answered weakly.

"Hold on a moment and I'll get you free."

"No-o-o!" he yelled.

Maggie turned but too late. She was thrown to the floor face down, a knee was planted firmly in the small of her back as her hands were pulled behind her back and firmly tied. While he worked, the man tying her kept shouting something in Spanish, and after a moment or two another man's voice answered him. She became aware that the second man had entered the room when the two of them lifted and dragged her to the far corner next to an old woodstove, tied her ankles together and roped them to the legs of the stove. She only got a glimpse of the men as they ran out the door. The next thing she heard was Oscar barking. He gave a yelp and then in the silence that followed she heard the sound of her car starting up. *Oscar! He'll be terrified!*

FIONA WAS WAITING FOR Nat when he pulled into the motel parking lot at six-thirty the next morning. As he opened his car door, she ran toward him.

"Why weren't you here? Maggie insisted on going to the police and the kidnappers said not to do that. Gordon's going to be killed and it will be your fault! I've only got twelve hours left to get the money to them."

"Calm down. Just calm down, Fiona. Maggie and I have it all under control."

"I told her to come back here last night and report to me, and she didn't come! What am I paying you people for?"

Nat returned to his car. "I'm going to pick Maggie up right now and we'll get in touch with you as soon as possible." He backed the car around and headed for the Apple Orchard B&B. When he pulled into the Rinaldi's yard, Maggie's car was not in its usual place, but the smell of bacon and fresh bread as he opened the kitchen door made him realize how hungry he was.

"Good morning, Nat," Bianca greeted him. "Your good lady is not up yet. Would you like to call her?" She smiled mischievously.

"But her car's not out there."

"She must have been up really early," Bianca said. "I've been up since five and I didn't see her go out."

He bounded up the stairs and threw open Maggie's bedroom door. But neither Maggie nor Oscar were in the room. He raced down the stairs. "She's not there! Are you sure she came back last night?"

"I don't know. She said she was going to see Reverend Bicknell. I didn't see her come home because Alonso and I went to bed early. We're sending a load of apples to the packing house this morning."

"Phone him."

Bianca grabbed the phone book and started searching for the number. Nat picked up the phone and waited until she read it out to him. "Reverend? Did Maggie Spencer come to see you last night? . . . What time did she leave? .

. .Did she say where she was going?. . .What? Are you sure about that?"

When he put the phone down, Bianca asked anxiously, "What did he say?"

"Bicknell thinks that she went to the Herrmanns." As he headed for the door, he stormed, "Damn you, Maggie! I've told you over-and-over not to go off on your own like this."

Nat's old Chevy pulled up in front of the Herrmanns' house in a cloud of dust and he raged up to the front door. To his surprise it was open and he could hear Rosa Herrmann crying. Pushing the door fully open, he rushed into the room where Peter Herrmann lay on the floor, his back propped up against the sofa. His nose was streaming blood, and the flesh around his left eye was cut and swollen. Rosa was kneeling beside him, wailing.

"What's happened?" Nat bent and helped the man to his feet and onto a chair before examining the damage to his face. "He's okay, Mrs. Herrmann. He's just been knocked around a bit. Who did this?" he demanded.

"Those two horrible men came back and started yelling at Peter in Spanish. They wanted $50,000! And when Peter wouldn't give them any money, they hit him!" Rosa burst into another torrent of tears.

"So why did they demand money?" Nat asked.

"I don't kno-o-ow," she wailed. "They said Adam cheated them. How could my son cheat them of all that money? Where would he get it? He was only a school boy."

But Nat had a pretty good idea where he got it. "Get your husband a wet towel or some ice." As soon as she left the room, he leaned over the man who was now holding his hands up to his face in an attempt to stem the flow of blood. "You sonofabitch," he snarled, "you have a lot to answer for! What have you done with my Maggie?"

"Who?" Herrmann asked groggily.

Nat grabbed him by his shirt front. "My partner, Maggie Spencer. She came to see you last night. What have you done with her?"

"Maggie? I don't know anybody named Maggie. . ."

When Rosa reappeared with the wet towel, Nat turned on her. "Where's Maggie?" he yelled.

"She hasn't been here," Rosa protested as she tried to get past him to wipe the blood from her husband's face. "The only people who've been here are those two men who did this to Peter. I told you—they wanted money!"

"So why do they want money from you, Herrmann?" Nat demanded, pulling the man roughly to his feet.

"I swear I don't know. I've never seen them before."

"I don't believe you. Your son was mixed up in some kind of drug deal and you are, too." He stalked to the door. "You're in a lot of trouble. I'm going to the police."

"No, wait!" Herrmann yelled. "They'll come back and kill us both."

Nat continued out the door and ran to his car, but he only drove up the road as far the beach access where he sat in the car for a moment, thinking. Then opening the door, he stepped out onto the sand and ran quickly back along the beach to the Hermann's gate. But he was too late. The shed door was now wide open and so was the trapdoor in the floor. An empty cashbox lay beside it. Nat heard the sound of a car starting up and realized that Herrmann was making his escape. Racing around the side of the house, he was just in time to see the blue Buick LeSabre tearing up the road.

Rosa stood on the path leading to the street wringing her hands and calling plaintively after him. "Peter! Come back! Don't leave me! Please, Peter, don't leave me. . ."

Nat began running up the road as fast as his bulk would allow, but Rosa clung to the sleeve of his jacket. "Make him come back," she cried. "Make him come back!"

"Let go," he said, stopping to unlock her fingers. "I'm going after that sonofabitch!"

"I'm coming with you!"

"No, let go," he said, pulling loose from her. At his car he unlocked the door and a moment later his old Chevy was roaring up to the T-junction. When he reached the highway, he looked right and left. "Which way would that bugger go?" He turned north and put his foot hard on the gas, but once he had rounded the bend where he could see the highway for miles ahead, there was no sign of the blue Buick LeSabre sedan. He swerved into a lookout over the lake, spun the car around and headed south at top speed.

"Where the hell are you, Maggie?"

He hadn't gone ten miles when he heard the siren, and looking up into his rear view mirror, he saw the flashing lights.

CHAPTER EIGHTEEN

"You're causing us a lot of trouble, Mrs. Spencer." The face of the man who bent over to test Maggie's bindings was covered by a black bandana. "Sorry we haven't time for a chat, but you've only got yourself to blame for being in this situation. You're very tiresome."

"My partner knows where I am," Maggie answered defiantly.

"Oh, I think not. But looking on the bright side, we should be able to recoup some of our missing money by getting him to part with a hefty ransom for you, too."

He laughed then turned to say something in fluent Spanish to the two men behind him. Both were masked, but she was pretty sure she was looking at Mateo and Rafael. They weren't too happy with whatever he said because one of them yelled back at him and pulled out a gun. She shrank back into the corner, but the boss man reached over, pushed the man's gun down and barked something more in Spanish.

Then he turned back to Maggie. "My friend here is suggesting that a quick bullet would resolve our problem of what to do with you. I've got to admit that he may have a point, but I think we'll try the ransom first."

Though Maggie found the two Spanish-speaking thugs scary, it was the faintly familiar, steely voice of their boss that scared her the most.

He turned to where Gordon was huddled. "As for you, boy, it's time for you to write another note to your devoted sister." Again he spoke in rapid Spanish, and one of the men untied Gordon's hands and thrust a pen and a notepad at him.

"SO WHAT'S THIS ALL ABOUT?" Sergeant Allen leaned back in his chair.

The uniformed cop who was holding fast to Nat's arm announced, "This guy has the fanciest excuse I've ever heard for speeding. He insists his partner has been kidnapped and is going to be killed."

"It's Maggie! They've got Maggie!"

"So you must be Southby. And what makes you so sure they've got Mrs. Spencer?"

"She's been out all night," Nat answered. "Her car's missing and so is Oscar."

"Oscar?"

"Her dog. She never goes anywhere without him. And the last person to see her was Anthony Bicknell around seven o'clock last night."

"Where was this?"

"At his house."

"Why did she go to see Bicknell?" Sergeant Allen nodded at the uniformed cop, dismissing him, and the man let go of Nat's arm and left the room.

"To find out how his cassock got into that rowboat. And, incidentally, he has absolutely no idea how it got there. But he said that Maggie mentioned that she was going to talk to the Herrmanns."

"The Herrmanns? Why would she go to see them?"

"Because of the haul of drugs you found in that rowboat, of course! I've just been to see the bloody Herrmanns, but they insist Maggie hasn't been there. In fact, when I got there, Herrmann had just been viciously attacked by two thugs demanding $50,000. Oh, and his wife said these guys spoke Spanish. They apparently told Herrmann that his kid had cheated them. My guess is it was payment for that cocaine."

"So you think the kid kept part of the payoff," Allen replied thoughtfully.

"Yes, I'm sure of it."

"And when he didn't produce the full amount, they killed him?"

"Right. And I'm pretty sure I know where the boy hid the money," Nat said, and he recounted the story of Peter Herrmann escaping in his car and how he had found the trap-door and the empty cash box. "So if that money was there," he continued, "Peter Herrmann has it now. So we need to find him quick because I'm damned sure he knows what's happened to Maggie."

"But all of this is just conjecture, Mr. Southby. Just because the man took off in a hurry doesn't mean he's guilty of anything. Or that he has anything to do with your missing part—"

There was a knock on the door and Fiona, quickly followed by the duty constable, pushed into the room.

"Sorry, sir. But she insisted she has to see you immediately."

Allen jumped to his feet. "What's happened now, Miss Phelps?"

But Fiona had spotted Nat, and she screamed into his face, "You'll have to do something to find my son now! They've got your precious Maggie, too!" And she handed a scrap of paper to an ashen-faced Nat.

Sis. They are now demanding $150,000 for me and a lady called Mrs. Spencer. They will contact you time and place for drop-off. They mean business.

CHAPTER NINETEEN

Maggie looked round the bare room and shuddered. As the cabin was shaded by the orchard trees, not much of the late afternoon sun penetrated through the single window, but even in the pale light she could see that the boy on the bunk had a mass of cuts and bruises on his face and arms. *Must have got those when his car crashed,* she thought.

"Those dudes are going to kill us, aren't they?" he said in a hopeless voice. "There's no way my mom can come up with that kind of bread. And they already killed Adam . . ."

Bread? Maggie thought. *Oh, of course, he means money.* "Don't worry, Gordon," she said. "My partner will rescue us."

"Your partner?"

"I'm a private investigator, Gordon. Your mother hired my partner and me to find you. I've been in tighter spots than this, and he's always come through for me."

"I'm not a kid, you know," he answered forlornly, "so you don't have to lie to me. There's no way your partner's gonna find us here, and that dude said if my mom goes to the police, they're gonna waste me."

This boy, Maggie thought, *has seen too many gangster movies.* She glanced over at him in time to see him blinking back tears.

"I guess my Mum's pretty worried," he said.

"Yes, she's very worried, and that's why she hired us. But we're going to get out of this just fine." She would need to keep the boy talking to distract him from their predicament. "Now tell me what happened, Gordon. What made you go to Summerland with Adam Herrmann?"

He shrugged. "It sounded like a gas."

"But you knew the Herrmanns are a pretty dodgy family, didn't you?"

"Yeah, but I've had it living with my grandparents. Don't do this, don't do that. Always on my case. You don't know what it's like!"

"So how did you get to know Adam?"

"He was my lab partner at Byng. He was different, y'know—kinda hip. . . Anyway, my mom bought me the car, so Adam said why don't I drive us to Summerland."

"But you knew his family was into drugs?"

"Nah, I didn't know that then." He was quiet for a few moments. "Adam and I were pretty tight, y'know, but he didn't tell me they were selling drugs."

"When did you realize something funny was going on there?"

"I didn't. We spent most of the time swimming and lying on the beach. We drove around in my car, too— went all the way to Vernon one day. And the Hermanns have this cool rowboat and once we rowed it right across the lake. . ."

"To Naramata."

"Yeah. How did you know that?"

"That's when you met the Reverend Bicknell?"

"Is he the guy at the church?"

"Yes. He told me he had met two nice young men who were interested in his church."

"Yeah. It's nothing much, but Adam kept asking him questions about it."

"So what made you guys go back there?"

"I was supposed to drive back to the Coast on Friday but Adam said why don't I stay. His old man and old lady had gone to Calgary, and he had to do this job for his dad. He had to row over to Naramata again, and if I went with him, I could help him row. He says his dad was gonna make it worth our while, and I could do with the bread . . ."

"What time did you go over there?"

"Adam says we have to wait until it's dark. . ."

"So what time was that?"

"About midnight, I think, when we got there. So we beach the boat, I get out and Adam hands me the case of beer."

"Beer?"

"Yeah. Cause he said we're going to have to wait a while."

"And then what happened?"

"I follow him up the path to the road and we go round to the side door of the church."

"How did you get in?"

"Adam slipped the lock when we were there before, and the old boy didn't notice. We go into this back room that has a couple of big chairs and a desk in it."

"The vestry," Maggie said. "And you sat there and drank?"

He nodded. "Yeah. So a couple of beers later and I'm dancing round the room wearing this black cape thing I found in the closet when somebody starts banging on the side door. I think it's gotta be the Reverend, but Adam tells me it's the dudes he's come to meet, and he tells me to hide somewhere and keep quiet. So I go into the closet, and I can hear him talking to these dudes—they're talking in Spanish, and I didn't even know Adam knew how to speak Spanish. And they're smoking because I can smell it. And then it goes quiet." He was silent for a moment and then added, "That's when they must have gone down to the boat and loaded those packages into it."

"But they came back to the church?"

"Yeah. About ten or fifteen minutes later. They come through that back room and go into the main part of the church, and pretty soon I hear them shouting. So I sneak along the passage until I can see into the church." Gordon's voice faltered.

"What did you see, Gordon?"

"Oh, God, it was awful. . . Adam. . . One of them hit him on the head with something. . . I saw them do it. . . There was blood everywhere. I got the hell out of there, and I ran along the road 'til I came to the path down to the beach. Then I hear those two Spanish guys right behind me. I push the boat out into the water, and I'm fitting the oars into the oarlocks when they catch up to me."

"But you got away. . ."

"I'm rowing away and they wade into the water right after me. One of them fires a shot, but he misses and I duck down and keep rowing. "

"So who started the fire?"

"What fire?"

"The church burned down. That's how they discovered your friend's body."

"Burned down!"

"Yes. The fire started in a waste-basket in the vestry."

He was silent for a moment and then said, "Those Spanish guys were smoking. Maybe they did it."

"So you crossed the lake and got into your car. . ," Maggie prompted.

"Yeah, I get to the other side and I jump into my car and I take off for the Coast. And I roar through Penticton, but then I see this car coming up fast behind me and I think it's the fuzz, but it's these Spanish guys, and they keep following and bumping into the back end of my car, and next thing I know I'm flying and my car goes end-over-end. And when it stops, I'm a mess. . ."

"Which explains all your cuts and bruises."

"So then these two guys drag me outta my car and brought me here." He paused for quite a few seconds this time. "Do you know what happened to my car? I guess it's a write-off . . ."

"No, but it's pretty badly damaged. It was towed away but I'm sure you'll be able to drive it again."

"If those dudes don't waste us first." Neither of them spoke for a few minutes.

"Why don't you try and get some sleep?"

The boy didn't answer her, just leaned back against the wall and closed his eyes.

He may talk big, but he's only a scared kid, she thought as she wriggled around until she could sit with her back against the wall. It was very quiet now, and she wondered where the three men had gone. She closed her eyes, and then suddenly opened them again, certain she heard a dog barking in the distance. *Could that possibly be Oscar?*

CHAPTER TWENTY

"Henny?" Nat asked when she picked up the phone.

"Oh, Mr. Nat! You haf just caught me. I was going to lock the office and go home."

"Is George there?"

"Mr. George left early. He say he is going on stake-out."

"Stake-out? What stake-out? Is this something to do with the Sowerby case?"

"I don't know, Mr. Nat. He investigates many times at night."

"Tell him I will call him in the morning."

As he put the phone down, Nat said to himself, *Well, George said he thought Sowerby was lying, and I guess he's following up on it. Good old George—always thorough!*

MAGGIE WOKE WITH A START. It seemed she had only closed her eyes, but now moonlight was seeping through the window. *What had wakened her?* Then she heard the sound again—a scratching at the door and whimpering. Oscar!

"Oscar! I'm in here."

There was a yelp accompanied by a stream of Spanish, the door was thrust open and the two thugs walked in. There was no sign of Oscar.

"Where's my dog, you bastards?"

There was no answer from either of them. Even in the moonlight Maggie could see that neither man was wearing a bandana over his face, and she was able to confirm what she had suspected: they were Bianca's two apple pickers. *And they're not worried about us seeing them!* She knew this was a bad sign, and when one of them removed the rope that fastened her ankles to the stove leg, she tried to bolt for the door but sprawled headlong when the other man stuck out his foot to trip her.

"What are you doing?" Gordon yelled as the first man began untying his ankles then yanked him off the bed. The reply was a vicious slap across his face and a gag roughly shoved into his mouth.

"Leave him alone!" Maggie yelled as she struggled to get up off the floor.

The thug only turned from Gordon and slapped her so hard that she fell back to the floor. The blow cut her lip, and the blood mixed with the salty tears of frustration that streamed down her face. Before she could get to her feet again, the thug sat on her and thrust a gag into her mouth and a blind over her eyes.

Oh, my God, they're going to kill us! Where are you, Nat?

First Maggie and then Gordon was pushed out of the cabin and stuffed into the back seat of a car. *It smells like my Morris Minor,* she thought. It rocked violently as one of the men climbed into the front seat. When the engine came to life, the driver rammed the car into gear. *It is my car! I'd know the sound of that engine anywhere.*

If Maggie could have looked back through the rear window, she would have seen Oscar following them down the long drive through the orchard and out onto the main road. But the car was too fast for him and he was eventually left behind, crouching and whimpering in the dead grass at the side of the road as the car disappeared from sight.

Maggie figured they had been on the road for a little over an hour when the driver geared down and the car began to climb. Now she realized that the road was also winding as it climbed because every so often she and the boy slid from one side of the back seat to the other. When at last they stopped climbing, there was another half-hour of travel on a paved road before the car turned onto a rutted gravel road and stopped. The front passenger door opened and the second man jumped in, greeting the first one in Spanish, and the car started up again, this time going uphill, sometimes skidding on turns, sometimes bouncing over rocks, sometimes grinding to a halt before the driver attacked a bend in the track from another angle. Once the front passenger got out and pushed when the car got stuck. Several times the car bumped and slid downhill into a steep gulley of some kind, and once she heard the sound of splashing water before the car ground uphill again, on and on and up and up.

The thug who had tied the rope binding Maggie's wrists hadn't been all that thorough, and on the long drive she worked her hands up and down against the knots, and they finally began to loosen. Suddenly the car skidded to a stop on the gravel, and when the doors were flung open, Maggie was immediately dragged out and pulled to her feet. She stumbled and fell as she was pushed ahead of her captor, but he just yanked her upright again and pushed her ahead of him. They came to a sudden stop and she heard a wooden door being banged open and then she was thrown onto a rough wooden floor. Seconds later the boy landed on top of her. The door slammed shut and to her dismay she heard her beloved car drive away.

CHAPTER TWENTY-ONE

Bianca insisted that Nat stay at the B&B until there was some news on Maggie's disappearance. "You can use her room," she had added, handing him clean towels. "After all, there's nothing you can do until the morning."

He agreed, even though he felt guilty trying to sleep instead of being somewhere, anywhere, looking for her. He tossed and turned until nearly morning when, utterly exhausted, he fell into a deep, nightmarish sleep.

The knock on the door woke him with a start, and he lay momentarily on his back trying to think where he was. Then, realizing by the smell of her perfume that he must be in Maggie's bed, he reached out to touch her, only to have the past day's events rush through his mind. "Oh, God, where are you, Maggie?"

Bianca knocked again before opening the door. "Here's a cup of coffee. It's eight o'clock and the kids have just left for school," she said, placing the cup on the night table. "Breakfast will be ready by the time you're up and dressed."

"I don't suppose there's any news?"

She shook her head.

In the bathroom as Nat reached for his razor, he thought, *I must call George again and catch up with what's happening in the Sowerby case.*

"Good morning," Alonso said, looking up from his breakfast as Nat entered the kitchen.

As Nat sat down, Bianca put a plate of eggs and bacon in front of him. But it was a silent meal as their collective thoughts were on Maggie's kidnapping, and after a few bites Nat pushed his plate away.

"Will you have more coffee, Nat?" Bianca said, going to the stove to get the coffee pot. At that moment there was a loud knocking on the kitchen door. They all froze. More bad news? The knock was repeated as Alonso hurried to open it.

Major Stroud stood at the door holding a limp Oscar in his arms. "I'm sure this little fellow is Mrs. Spencer's dog," he said, entering the kitchen.

"Oscar!" Nat rushed to take the almost lifeless dog out of the major's arms. "Where did you find him?"

"In the grass across the road from my orchard," Stroud answered. "The poor old thing was just lying there at the side of the road, and I recognized him immediately because I met Mrs. Spencer walking him on the beach one day. I can't imagine how he ended up so far from here. Mrs. Spencer must have been looking everywhere for him. Is she about?"

"You haven't heard?" Bianca asked as she wrapped a huge towel around the dog. "She's missing!" She turned to Nat. "Here, Nat, put him in his basket and I'll warm some milk with a little brandy for him."

"What do you mean 'missing'?" the major demanded. "The last I heard she was looking into the tragic death of that boy who was killed in the church fire."

Oscar looked up into Nat's face and weakly wagged his tail.

"If only you could talk, Oscar," Nat said, placing the warm milk near the animal's nose. "Come on, old boy. Drink it up."

"Sit down and have some coffee, Major," Bianca said, always the hostess. "This is Nat, Maggie's partner, and he's helping the police find her. She and a boy—a friend of the one who was killed—have both been kidnapped."

"Kidnapped! Here in Naramata? That's ridiculous. That sort of thing doesn't happen here." He turned to Nat, who was kneeling on the floor beside the dog. "Is there anything I can do?"

Nat shook his head as he gently pushed Oscar's nose into the milk. "Come on, Oscar." The dog took a few laps then lay back on his bed and closed his eyes. Nat looked up at the major. "Thank you for bringing him back."

"Only too glad to help," he replied. "Must get going. . ." He walked to the door then turned back. "Mrs. Spencer drives a red car, doesn't she?"

"Why?" Nat asked. "Have you seen it?"

"Yesterday. Of course, I could have been mistaken— but there aren't many small red cars around here."

"For God's sake, man, where did you see it?"

"Just outside Penticton. I was on my way back from visiting friends, and she passed me heading north toward Summerland."

"You saw Maggie driving *north*?" Bianca asked.

"Are you sure it was her car?" Nat asked.

"Well, I'm pretty certain. But of course I could be wrong. . ."

"So Bicknell was right," Nat said. "She *did* go to Summerland to see the Herrmanns!" He turned back to the major. "But how did Oscar get to your orchard?"

"Yes, that's certainly odd, isn't it?" the major answered as he opened the back door. "Anyway, I have to go. I hope you find your partner safe and sound, Mr. Southby."

"Wait. . ."

But the major was already heading for his car. As he climbed into it, he waved and closed the door.

Nat stood on the porch staring at the car as it drove off.

Bianca, clearing away the breakfast plates, said, "He's such a nice man."

"Nice man," Alonso repeated.

"No," Nat said, shaking his head. "There's something not quite right about that man."

"What's not right?" Bianca asked. "The major is very well thought of here."

"Yes," Alonso agreed. "We don't have cabins and our apple pickers stay in his cabins for free."

"Yes," Bianca repeated. "He's a very good neighbour."

"But," Nat said, "how does he know my name?"

"I introduced you," Bianca answered.

"You introduced me as Nat, and he called me Mr. Southby." He headed for the telephone. "Which one of your neighbours drives a wood-panelled station wagon?"

"None, as far as I know," Bianca answered, looking enquiringly at Alonso.

"Those two Mexican guys who pick for us—they got one," he said.

"You mean Rafael and Mateo?" Bianca asked her husband.

Alonso nodded.

"Where do they stay?" Nat asked as he started dialing.

"Major Stroud's," she said, "but I think they've gone home now. They only come to us at the end of the season for a couple of weeks." She turned to Alonso. "When was the last time you saw their car?"

Alonso looked stricken. "Two, maybe three days ago. But the Major said Maggie's car was going to Summerland. . ."

"I think he's lying," Nat said. He spoke into the phone. "Sergeant Allen please. . . yes, I can hold." He turned back to Bianca and Alonso and asked, "Where is Stroud's place?"

"He has sign at his gate," Alonso said, pointing south toward Penticton. "Ashford Apple Orchards."

"Can you see his cabins from the road?"

"No, no. There're way far back," Alonso answered, waving in the direction of the hills to the east.

"Yes," Bianca cut in. "There's a very, very long driveway that goes all the way to the cabins. But I can't believe the major would have something to do with Maggie's disappearance."

"If the cabins are as isolated as you say," Nat said, "it's possible he wouldn't even be aware of what's going on there." Then he turned back to the phone. "Sergeant Allen, it's Southby. I've got some new information. We're looking for Maggie and the boy in the wrong place. . ."

CHAPTER TWENTY-TWO

Maggie freed her hands from the rope, pulled off the dirty piece of rag that was blinding her and the gag from her mouth and looked around the bare room. Dawn wasn't far away as she could see a faint light seeping through the small window, and she could hear the sound of birds waking up.

Gordon, lying huddled against the far wall where their captors had dumped him, moaned.

"It's okay, Gordon," she said, crawling over to the boy and whipping the gag from his mouth.

"I thought they were going to kill us," he said in a shaky voice as she removed the blindfold from his eyes.

Tears slid down his face as she struggled with the rope binding his hands, and she tried to think how Barbara or Midge would have coped with all this at his age. Probably not much better than this unfortunate boy, she thought. "They must've thought you were a real threat to them," she said and laughed in the hope of breaking the tension, "because they made a much better job of tying you up than me. Ah, there you go," she added as she slipped the rope from the boy's wrists. "Now rub your hands together and get the circulation going."

"Where are we?"

"I have no idea," she answered, getting to her feet, "but we must be well away from civilization because I can't hear any cars. And those bloody men have driven off in my car and left us in this godforsaken cabin." She walked to the door, and finding that it opened to her touch, cracked it open and peeped out. To her relief there was no one waiting outside to kill them as they stepped out, and she opened the door wider. "But to top it off, it's raining," she lamented.

Gordon hauled himself to his feet and joined her in the doorway. He hugged himself as he looked out onto the dreary landscape of dripping trees that appeared like ghosts in the misty morning light. "Do you think they left us something to eat?"

Maggie shook her head. "I doubt it." She turned to look around the cabin. There was a rickety table and the remains of a bunk bed against one wall. She looked up at the water dripping through the holes in the roof.

"What are we going to do for food," the boy moaned, "and how are we going to get home?"

"At the moment I don't have answers for either of those questions, Gordon," she said briskly. "We'll have to wait until it's lighter outside, and then perhaps we'll have a better idea of where we are." But Maggie knew they were in a very bad way. Obviously the two men had no intention of coming back for them, Nat and the Penticton police would have no idea where they were, and she was pretty sure that after the thugs had dumped them here, they would have escaped across the international border while the going was good. But what about the real boss of the operation? His voice still nagged at her. She was sure she had heard it before.

For the next hour Maggie and the boy sat side-by-side against the wall, waiting until it was light enough to venture outside. Neither of them was wearing clothes suitable for roaming very far in the rain, but Maggie thanked her lucky stars that she had given up wearing skirts while at the Orchard B&B. Fortunately, though her jacket, shirt and slacks were only summer weight, her shoes were quite sturdy. Gordon, a typical teenager, was wearing jeans, T-shirt, a light jacket and running shoes, which like Maggie's attire, was only great while the sun was shining. Now if he would just stop reminding her with his whining about food how hungry *she* was!

When it was finally light enough for them to venture outside, they could see that the cabin sat alone on a tiny piece of cleared land with a little creek running beside it. They knelt down and, cupping their hands, scooped water into their mouths.

"Not bad," Maggie said. "I've tasted better but at least it's water."

She stood up and set off, dodging from puddle to puddle, down a rutted path that led toward an equally rutted but now overgrown logging road. "Come on, Gordon," she said without turning to see if he was following. She had already spotted tire marks where the two men had turned her car around for their return journey down the steep hill, and it was these tracks that were going to lead them back to civilization.

"What's that stuff?" Gordon said, pointing.

She walked over to the small pile at the side of the logging road and crouched down to have a closer look. "It's Oscar's blanket!" Kneeling down on the wet pine needles, she picked it up. "Those bloody men have dumped all my things out of the car. Look at this!" Under the blanket was the old sweater she always kept on the back seat for emergencies, Oscar's chewed rubber ball and her handbag. Naturally the money was gone from her bag, but they had left her lace handkerchief, address book and lipstick. But what really puzzled her were the car registration and licence plates lying at the bottom of the pile. "Why would they throw these away?"

"Come on," Gordon said. "Let's keep going."

"Just a minute," she said, pocketing the car registration. "I've got to collect my stuff."

"Come on," he said again. "We've gotta find food."

Brushing a wet strand of hair from her eyes, she picked up her handbag and the licence plates and staggered to her feet. "Okay, Gordon. Let's go."

"Not so fast, Missy."

Slowly she turned to where Gordon was standing with a look of terror on his face. Maggie had heard of hillbillies, and there was one in the flesh right behind Gordon. Topped by long unkempt hair and scraggly whiskers, this apparition was wearing a ragged coat held together with rope and dirty trousers stuffed into muddy rubber boots, and he was pointing a shotgun straight at Gordon's head.

"What the hell do you think you're doing?" Maggie demanded.

"Huh! A spunky one. Git over here or I'll plug the kid."

"Don't be ridiculous. Step away from him, Gordon."

The man swung his gun from pointing at Gordon to pointing into the nearby trees and pulled the trigger. "I said git over here! I'm a crack-shot and the next one will git yer."

"Please do what he says," Gordon pleaded.

Maggie gritted her teeth and moved to stand beside the boy.

"Now walk nice and easy up the hill. Mind, I've got me gun on yer."

NAT SAT IN HIS car with a somewhat recovered Oscar on his lap at the entrance to the major's orchard where Sergeant Allen had agreed to meet him. It had been a couple of hours since his call to the police station, so Nat was frantic by the time the sergeant arrived, and he hurried over to his car.

"I know you're worried," Allen said, "but we can't go in there and accuse the man just because he brought the dog back."

"I know that," Nat replied. "But at least let's have a look at those cabins."

"Okay. I see your point. But you let me do the talking. Understood?"

Nat followed the police car up the long drive to the major's very large house. The heavy oak door was opened by the major's housekeeper, and she kept the two of them waiting on the doorstep while she went to find him.

"Now what's this all about?" Stroud asked irritably. "I've brought your dog back—what else do you want?"

"We'd like to take a look at your cabins if you don't mind," Allen replied.

"Whatever for? They're empty. My last two apple pickers left a couple of days ago."

"There's a possibility that Mrs. Spencer and probably Gordon Phelps have been held captive in one of those cabins."

"Captive! Don't be ridiculous. I've never heard such nonsense."

"All the same, I'd appreciate it if you would let us take a look at them."

"Don't you have to have a warrant for that kind of thing?"

"I can get one if you insist, but we only need to have a look around. We think that, probably unknown to you, some of the migrant workers are responsible for the kidnappings and the demands for ransom money."

"It seems to me that you're grasping at straws. Those two wouldn't have the intelligence to kidnap anyone and demand a ransom—they can hardly speak English. Anyway, you're welcome to have a look. None of the cabins are locked."

The major was right. The first of the six dreary cabins they came to was unlocked and empty. It had the barest of necessities—a worn wooden table and three chairs, a sink and drain board, a wood stove and two double bunks.

As they came out of the cabin, Nat saw Oscar pawing frantically at the car window. He ran over and opened the door, and the dog erupted from the car and hightailed it for the third cabin in the row, barking shrilly. By the time they caught up with him he was scratching desperately at the door. As soon as Nat opened it, the dog ran straight to the pot-bellied stove and began sniffing at the floor beside it. Then whining, he ran back and forth between the stove and Nat.

"We've got our answer," Allen said, watching the dog's antics. "Your Maggie has definitely been kept in this cabin—and forcibly by the look of those pieces of rope." He pointed. "Let's go and have another little chat with the major."

"That's all very well," Nat answered worriedly, "but where is she now?"

This time Nat and the Sergeant confronted the major inside his house.

"You have the audacity to accuse me of kidnapping Mrs. Spencer and that boy? You'd better be careful, Sergeant Allen. Do you realize that I could have you dismissed from the force?"

"I'm not accusing you of anything at the moment," Allen replied. "But how could you not know what your pickers were up to? It's obvious that both the boy and the woman have been held captive in one of your cabins."

"I allow my pickers to use those cabins for the season. All I'm interested in is their ability to pick and pack fruit. What they do while they're living there is their affair. And I repeat," and here the major poked the sergeant in the chest, "you have no evidence of any kidnapping, and even if there was, you have nothing to connect me to it. Please leave my house immediately, and rest assured your superiors will hear about this. . . this outrage."

As the sergeant climbed into his car, Nat said, "I've got to let Miss Phelps know what's happened."

"What is there to tell?" the sergeant answered. "Just that the dog got all excited when we entered a picker's cabin? Major Stroud is quite right—the dog's behaviour is all the evidence we have that your partner and the boy were held captive there." He sat back with a pensive look.

"If Maggie was in that cabin," Nat said, "then what's happened to her car? You know it's bright red so it's not an easy car to hide."

"Do you know the make and the licence number?"

"Wait a minute. . ." He paused to gather his thoughts. "It's a Morris Minor, and I think Maggie bought it new about five years ago, so that makes it a 1957 model, but the licence number. . .um. . . I know it starts with PJ because I teased her about pyjamas." He closed his eyes. "PJ 787!"

"Okay." Sergeant Allen reached for his radio phone. "And while we're at it, we'll put out an APB on that wood- panelled station wagon as well."

"I'VE ALWAYS WANTED ME own woman," the man said, standing back to admire Gordon's knot-making handi-work.

Maggie cringed as he leaned over her and ran a dirty hand down her cheek. Here she was, tied up again—this time to a rickety kitchen chair—with this horrible man pointing his shotgun at a teary-eyed Gordon as he gave the boy explicit instructions on knot-making.

"Let me introduce meself, milady," he said, bowing to her. "Livingstone Stanley Gibbs. Me mum was into ex-plorers," he explained. "Dr. Livingstone and some geezer named Stanley. They discovered Africa or somethin'."

"She had good taste," Maggie answered cryptically. "But why do I have to be tied up?"

"Because yer might make a run fer it. Ladies like you gen'rally run from me," he said philosophically. Then waving his shotgun, he turned to Gordon. "Yer ever shot squirrels, boy?"

"No," Gordon said. "I don't like guns."

"Well, if yer coming to live wiv me, boy, yer'll hafta larn. We'll leave yer mother here while we go get us some squirrels fer dinner."

"She's not my mother."

Livingstone Gibbs shrugged. "Yer girl friend then." He laughed drily at the boy's discomfort.

"Have you got anything to eat?" Gordon asked forlornly.

"Eat? 'Scuse me, fergot me manners. There be some stew in that there fryin' pan. Better give yer girlfriend some, too."

Gordon walked over to the pot-bellied stove and looked down at the glutinous mess in the big iron frying pan. It had a funny, rancid smell, but he was so hungry that he picked up a spoon from the littered table and tentatively ate some. God knows what was in it, but to his surprise it didn't taste all that bad. He turned to Maggie.

"Would you like some?"

She shook her head. "No thank you."

"Well, come on, boy," Gibbs said impatiently. "Let's go get us some critters."

"Do I have to?"

"Yep. Like I said, if yer goin' to be a son of mine, yer'll hafta larn to shoot."

As soon as they left, Maggie tried wriggling her fingers to see how tight Gordon had made the knots. She strained against the cord, but it didn't give in the slightest, and she knew she didn't have any time to waste trying to wriggle out of her bonds. But she could see a very wicked-looking boning knife among the litter on the nearby table, and after several tries she managed to stand up, and then, feeling like a large, clumsy snail, she shuffled with the chair still attached to her bottom toward the table. Now her only problem was to somehow turn the chair around so her hands could reach the knife. The first time she tried, the chair leg hit the table leg and tipped her onto her knees. It took two more tries before she managed to align herself with the knife. Then carefully she let the feet of the chair rest back on the floor and sank into the seat. She was fast becoming exhausted from lack of food and sleep and by her efforts to escape, and time was not on her side—there was no telling how soon that horrible old man would return.

One more try! She staggered to her feet, leaned back until she could feel the edge of the table and groped for the knife. She felt a sharp pain as her fingers found the blade, but she managed to turn the knife around until her fingers could close on the smooth handle. As she fell back into the chair, it rocked onto its four legs. To give herself more room to operate, she stood up again and shuffled away from the table, then sat down and began sawing at the cords behind her back that tied her to the chair.

MAGGIE WAS WAITING BEHIND the door for Livingstone Stanley Gibbs when he and Gordon returned. Fed up to the teeth with being pushed around and tied up, she felt no compunction whatsoever as she hit the man over the head with the black iron frying pan. Unfortunately for him, it still contained a fair amount of stew.

CHAPTER TWENTY-THREE

"You call yourself a detective?" Fiona shouted at Nat. "You actually found where those thugs have been holding my son, and he's disappeared again? You're the most incompetent man I've ever met!" She sat down on the bed and burst into tears.

Nat couldn't help sympathizing with the woman. He did feel inadequate. And not knowing where Maggie was being held was almost too much to bear.

"The good thing is that Maggie and Gordon are together," he said as gently as he could, "and if anyone can get them out of a bad situation, Maggie's the one." When Fiona didn't respond, he continued, "The sergeant has put out an APB on her car, so they won't get across the border—"

"Why would they want to take *her* car?" she interrupted him. "They've got a perfectly good station wagon, and they've probably already crossed the border in it and taken my son with them!"

"There's no reason for them to take Gordon with them," Nat told her patiently. What he didn't say was that the kidnappers may have killed both Gordon and Maggie before they fled when they realized they weren't going to get their money. Instead he continued, "But you're absolutely right about them using their own vehicle, and the

Sergeant has already put out an APB on it as well. But since Maggie's car is missing, there's a very good chance they're using it instead. . ."

An hour later when Nat called into the police station, the news the sergeant had to impart was all bad. "We couldn't give the Customs people a licence number for the station-wagon, but a car fitting that description with a couple of Mexicans in it passed through this morning." Then he cautioned, "That doesn't mean it was them because at this time of year dozens of old cars and trucks carrying migrant workers cross the border every day heading home."

"For God's sake, Allen, which border crossing was it?"

"Midway. It's not a very busy crossing so that's why they remembered the car."

"Where the hell is Midway?"

"About forty-five miles east of Osoyoos. And yes, before you ask, we're already searching that area for your partner's car."

"I can't just sit here and wait," Nat said, standing up and heading for the door. "I'm going to join the search. That car has to be somewhere."

"I can't stop you, Nat. But you realize finding her car won't tell us where they've taken her and the boy. That's pretty wild country and far too large a territory for us to search thoroughly."

"But finding her car will give us a clue where to start looking."

WHEN HE REPORTED BACK to Fiona Phelps on his way out of town, she said, "I'm coming with you, and I don't want any arguments." She grabbed her coat.

"I thought you would," he said as he led the way to his car, "but before we go, I need to know if you've had any more ransom letters."

"No, but I don't know what frightens me more—those terrible threatening letters or the silence."

Nat knew what she meant. "I think the man in charge of the drug racket has figured out he's not going to get any money out of you, Fiona, and by now he must know that Adam's father has fled with it, and he's probably gone after him." He opened the passenger door for her, and Oscar greeted them enthusiastically.

"For God's sake, you're not taking that damned dog with us, are you?" Fiona demanded.

"That damned dog, Fiona, is going to lead us to Maggie and Gordon!"

"IS HE DEAD?" Gordon asked.

"I really don't care," Maggie answered, looking down with distaste at Livingston Stanley Gibbs covered in congealed stew. "No," she added, "he's beginning to stir. We'd better tie him up." And she handed Gordon a piece of the rope she had cut off her own hands. "Here, you tie his hands and I'll get his feet."

It had been a long, long time since their host had bathed, and it was difficult to get this close to him, but the task was soon completed. "Now," she said, "let's get the hell out of here before he wakes up." She handed Gordon the shotgun. "Here, take this. We don't want him coming after us with this thing." She stepped cautiously over Livingstone Stanley Gibbs and out the door.

"What's in that rucksack?" Gordon asked as he followed her.

"Dinner courtesy of Mr. Gibbs," she said, slipping the straps over her shoulders. "Come on, Gordon! Step lively. Those ropes won't hold him for long. We're going home."

It was only a fifteen minute walk from Gibbs' cabin back to the derelict cabin where Rafael and Mateo had left them, and though she had no idea where they were, she knew they had to go downhill from there because she remembered her car's engine labouring as it had climbed. Fortunately, even though it had been raining since then and the track was slippery with fallen pine needles and treacherous with rivulets of rainwater, there were still traces of tire tracks.

They had been walking for nearly an hour when Gordon began lagging behind. "I'm starving. Please let's stop," he pleaded. "I need something to eat."

Maggie kept walking. "We've got to get more distance between us and that crazy man." She was worried that Livingston Stanley Gibbs would have untied himself by this time and be back on his feet and following them to get his shotgun back.

"Please," Gordon said again. "I'm so hungry."

"Okay. Ten minutes." Sitting with her back against a white pine, Maggie opened the rucksack and pulled out a can of corned beef. The knife cuts on her fingers were still bleeding, and she passed the can over to the boy. "Here," she said, "you open it, but be careful you don't twist the key off."

"Yes, Ma." Gordon actually gave a little chuckle as he clumsily opened the tin.

He actually made a joke, Maggie thought. *There's hope for him yet.* She delved inside the bag again and pulled out a half-loaf of very stale bread and the knife she'd used to cut her bindings. "Here," she said, "make us a couple of sandwiches."

The rain had stopped and apart from the dripping leaves the forest was uncannily quiet. *I'm sure we'd hear if Gibbs was after us,* she thought as she took a bite out of the uneven sandwich Gordon had made for her. She looked over to the boy and saw he'd already wolfed down his whole sandwich. "We'll save the rest for later," she said, taking the can of corned beef from him.

"Can't I just have a little bit more?" He looked longingly as she resolutely stowed it back into the rucksack.

"No, Gordon. We have to ration ourselves. God knows how long it will take us to get back to civilization." She struggled to her feet and then stood stock still. "What was that? Did you hear that noise?"

"No."

For a long minute they remained rigid as statues. Finally the boy whispered, "I don't hear anything."

"Shush." Maggie slung the bag back onto her shoulders. "Get up quietly. He's out there." She pointed back up the hill.

"It's just a deer or something," Gordon whispered back.

But Maggie wasn't taking any chances. "No talking," she whispered. "Keep to the side of the track, and try not to dislodge any stones."

NAT AND FIONA HARDLY said a word to each other as he drove to Midway, which turned out to be a small border town spread out just south of the point where the highway intersected the Kettle Valley Railway line. This was where Nat planned to start the search for Maggie's car, street-by-street, but Fiona had other ideas.

"Look," she insisted as he pulled into a side street to begin the search, "those men escaped over the border in their station wagon, so they must have left it near the border for a quick get-away."

"So?"

"So they would have left Maggie's car near the border, too."

Nat disagreed. "They may be illiterate thugs, Fiona, but they would have enough sense to abandon Maggie's car somewhere out of sight during the night and then walk to where they had stashed their own car. Then they would've crossed the border as soon as it opened in the morning." When he saw that she was determined to run the show, he added irritably, "Okay, Fiona, where do you want to start?"

"The border," she said.

So they started at the border and slowly worked their way back to the highway by driving up and down each street and cul-de-sac and into every long driveway and farmyard. They asked everyone they met if they had seen Maggie's car, but they were just as unsuccessful as the police had been before them. Nobody remembered seeing a little red car in recent days.

Finally, tired, discouraged and hungry, Nat said, "It's going to be dark in an hour. Let's find some place to eat before we head back."

"We can't just go back! We've got to find them!"

"Just because a wood-panelled station wagon crossed the border here doesn't mean it was the kidnappers' station wagon," he answered wearily. "There's half a dozen places they could have crossed. Or they could have abandoned their car and walked." Being with Fiona for such a long stretch was enough to make any patient man weary— and Nat wasn't a patient man. "I saw a café a couple of blocks over. "We'll eat and then find somewhere to stay for the night and start again in the morning."

AS THE SHADOWS LENGTHENED and evening came on, Maggie became obsessed with the thought that Gibbs was stalking them. When they heard yet another crackle of twigs on the hillside above them, Gordon tried to reassure her, grabbing her arm and whispering, "It's just a deer. If it was Gibbs, he would have shot at us by now."

Maggie turned and pointed to the gun he was carrying.

"Oh," he whispered. "I've got his gun, haven't I?"

"Exactly! Come on. Let's hide behind those bushes and wait for a bit. If it's him, we'll shoot him with his own weapon," she said. She spoke with bravado for the boy's benefit, but actually she was terrified at the very thought of shooting anything. She wasn't even sure she could.

They didn't have all that long to wait before they glimpsed a tall figure looming up between the trees. Seconds later they lost sight of the figure as if whoever it was had seen them and bent down to hide. Maggie, shaking like a leaf, took the gun from Gordon, raised it to her shoulder and aimed it where she thought the figure would reappear. But when it did, it was not Gibbs they saw. It was a huge black bear, rearing up on its hind legs and scenting the air. Gordon shrieked, turned and headed down the hill as fast as he could run, leaving Maggie facing the animal alone.

"Oh, my God!" she muttered. "I bet it's the corned beef! That damned animal has been following the smell." She dropped the gun, fumbled inside the rucksack, found the can with the rest of the corned beef and flung it with all her strength in the direction of the bear. She didn't wait to see if the animal went after it or if it was considering a much larger meal. She snatched up the gun and the ruck-sack and followed Gordon's retreating figure as fast as she could.

The trail branched several times, but at last she spotted the imprint of the boy's running shoes in the mud. "Gordon!" she yelled, and when he answered, she found him quite a way down the track, huddled against a tree stump, his arms around his knees.

"I thought the bear had got you," he breathed when he saw her coming down the trail.

"He smelled the corned beef—so I gave it to him."

"What are we going to eat now?"

"We won't starve. I pinched a couple of cans of sardines from Gibbs, too."

"I hate sardines. Why didn't you throw *them* at the bear?"

"I don't think bears know how to open sardine cans."

He gave a half-hearted chuckle.

"Come on, Gordon," she said, handing him the gun to carry. "Let's get as far away from here as we can before it gets really dark."

They walked for another half hour, stopping every few minutes to listen in case the bear was following them. As they walked, Gordon gradually opened up and told Maggie what it was like living with his mother, who was pretending to be his sister for appearances sake, and the two elderly grandparents who forced the pretence.

"It's not that I don't love them," he protested as they waded through a shallow creek. "I only wish Mum and I could live in a place of our own, you know, so I can ask my friends back. Especially now I'm going to university."

As Maggie listened to him, she thought back to her own two daughters' teen years. Both she and Harry had made sure that their girls' growing-up years were as happy as possible, and although he had changed from the man she'd had so much fun with at the beginning of their marriage to become a pretentious bore, she had to admit that he did love their daughters, and they loved him.

"Where the hell are we?"

She had been so engrossed in her thoughts of family that Gordon's sudden exclamation brought her up sharply. "What?"

"We've come to the end of the road," he said, pointing ahead. "Look!"

THEY HAD JUST COME around a curve, and about fifty feet ahead of them the overgrown logging road they had been following had come to a sudden end. The sliver of moon that slipped in and out of the black clouds overhead shone on a circular lake surrounded by trees and brush.

"We've taken a wrong turn," she said.

"Must've been back there where we met the bear," the boy said. "There were a couple of roads branching off . . ."

She felt like sitting down and having good cry, but he looked so dejected she had to mentally pull herself together. "Come on. Let's explore. There must be some way around it."

There wasn't. The lake was completely encircled by dense jack pine forest.

"We'll have to wait till it gets light," she said, and the two of them, tired and very hungry, settled on a small patch of pebbled beach and leaned against a large granite rock. *Probably left over from the ice age,* Maggie thought bitterly, *and someday when they find our bones here, they'll think we were a couple of Neanderthals.* She opened two cans of sardines and passed one to the boy.

Gordon, who seemed to have forgotten that he didn't like sardines, didn't even complain as he scooped up the oily fish with his fingers and crammed them into his mouth.

THE ONLY RESTAURANT THAT was open in Midway was a greasy spoon, and Nat and Fiona had to settle for hamburgers and fries. Their accommodation wasn't much better, and they didn't even say good-night as they slipped their respective keys into the locks of the side-by-side rooms they had been assigned in the dreary strip motel.

CHAPTER TWENTY-FOUR

Maggie and Gordon spent the night with their backs to the rock, Gordon cuddling Gibbs' shotgun, and the two of them huddling close together for warmth. Maggie tried to keep her thoughts centred on her cozy bed at home, all the while ignoring the rustlings and creakings issuing from the dark forest behind them. She even thought longingly of the warmth they might have gained from Oscar's smelly blanket they'd left behind at the side of the track. But the encounter with the bear continued to prey on her mind, and any idea of sleep was destroyed by the thought that the noises she was hearing in the forest were either the bear looking to see what else they had to feed him or Gibbs trailing them to get his shotgun back. On the one hand she hoped she hadn't killed him with the frying pan, but she was convinced that if he was alive, he would have freed himself by now and would be tracking them. And then she really would have to kill him.

The boy, a typical teenager, slept.

She waited until it was nearly dawn before gently disentangling herself from Gordon and struggling to her feet. Stretching her arms above her head, she looked around the stark landscape slowly taking shape around them. Thirst and a full bladder were her immediate concerns. After relieving herself behind a bush, she walked down to the edge of the lake, scooped up some of the icy water in her cupped hands and sniffed it—*brackish but drinkable*, she decided—and drank enough to quench her thirst. Then scooping up more water, she splashed it over her face before walking back to where Gordon still slept. She hated to wake him, but the sooner they made their way back along the track to the place where they met the bear and found the right way down the mountain the better.

IT WAS BARELY LIGHT when Nat rapped on Fiona's door with a steaming cardboard cup of coffee in his hand.

"Here's coffee to get you going," he said, handing her the cup. "We can get some breakfast at the same place we went to last night before we head back."

"I don't want breakfast," Fiona snapped, taking the cup from him. "I'll wait here for you. I suppose you've got some great idea where to look next."

He ignored the sarcasm. She looked as tired as he felt. He'd tossed and turned most of the night on the lumpy mattress worrying where Maggie could be, and he was sure Fiona hadn't slept well either, worrying about her son.

"I shouldn't be long. Give me your thermos and I'll have them fill it. And I'll buy some sandwiches for us to take along, too. Any particular kind you'd like?"

"Get whatever you like," she said shortly and closed her door.

Although it was only seven o'clock, the little restaurant was fairly full—mostly with men and women heading to work—and Nat had to make do with a stool at the counter.

"So where you heading?" the waitress asked, placing a plate in front of him loaded with the eggs, ham, sausage and home fries he had ordered.

"Not far," he replied, reaching for the ketchup. Then with one of his famous wild hunches, he said, "I don't suppose you've seen a small red car around here in the last day or so, have you?"

She shook her head. "Don't get out very much. You lost one?"

Nat nodded. "Kind of. My partner and her car have gone missing." He handed one of his crumpled business cards to her. "We think she was headed this way."

"Detective, eh? Don't have much call for detectives here." She turned to the man who had taken the stool next to Nat. "What do you want, Colin? The usual?"

"Yeah, Dixie. Just make sure the eggs are sunny-side-up this time, okay? And I want hash browns not fries." He turned to Nat. "What kind of a car is it?"

"Morris Minor. Have you seen it?"

"Yeah, I saw a red Morris Minor, but it wasn't a woman driving it. It was a couple of guys. Dark skin, black hair. Looked like casual workers, you know. Apple pickers. I noticed it because the car looked fairly new and not the usual rust-buckets those guys drive around in."

"When was this?"

"Yesterday."

"Do you remember what time?"

"Early in the morning. I was on my way in from Osoyoos after my week off." He paused and thought for a minute. "I guess it was around five. I work at the gravel pit up the road a ways." He hooked a thumb to the east.

"So this Morris Minor you saw was on the highway? Which way was it going?"

"No-no. It was parked just off one of those tracks that go up into the mountains north of here. I noticed it because one of the guys was out of the car and talking to the driver through the window. Looked to me they were arguing. Arms going all over the place."

"Could you show me where you saw them?"

"Nah, I'm heading to work and I'm late already, but you can't miss it. Just take the highway west toward Osoyoos for a mile or so, and it's the first track you come to. As I said, it goes 'way up into the mountains."

Nat left the restaurant without finishing his breakfast.

A half-hour later as he and Fiona sat in his car at the foot of the track, she snarled, "You can't drive up *there*! You're mad." She stepped out of the car and pointed up the track. "See! It's hardly wide enough for a little car like Maggie's Morris, let alone this heap of yours. And look at all the ruts and that stream pouring down the middle of it."

"I'm going to give it a try, Fiona," Nat answered her as patiently as he could. "This is the last place Maggie's car was seen, and that's good enough for me. Are you coming with me or not?"

Wordlessly she got back in the car. He gunned the engine and they started up the mountain.

But Fiona was right. Nat's old Chevy was no match for the narrow, rutted track. Reluctantly, with the help of his equally reluctant passenger directing him with many hand signals and impatient yells, Nat backed down to the highway again. After parking on the roadside as close to the overflowing ditch as he could, he slithered over the bench seat and onto the track.

"So what are you going to do now?" Fiona asked scathingly.

"Hike," he answered. "Come along, Oscar. Let's find Maggie."

"Hike? Are you crazy?"

Nat didn't bother to answer as, sidestepping the fast-running stream cascading down the middle of the track, he started up the mountain with Oscar running and sniffing the ground ahead of him. Neither of them looked back to see if Fiona was following.

"Nat, stop!"

When he kept plodding on, she caught up and grabbed the back of his jacket. "Look! Fresh tire tracks!"

He crouched down to inspect them. "It's Maggie's car all right. I'm sure of it."

They hurried on, Fiona labouring up the hill right beside Nat now, but they had only hiked another hundred feet when Oscar, who had raced ahead, gave a sharp bark.

"What is it, Oscar? What have you found?"

The dog had found Maggie's red Morris Minor pushed into a small clearing. Splattered with mud and badly scratched, it had been half-buried in bracken and bushes. The trunk lid, passenger and driver's doors were wide open to the elements.

Fiona rushed ahead to look inside. "It's empty!" she said.

Nat breathed a sigh of relief. He had been terrified of what they would find inside it.

IT HAD TAKEN MAGGIE quite a bit of persuasion to get Gordon going. He was hungry, thirsty and thoroughly miserable.

He's definitely not a morning person, she decided. "For God's sake, Gordon, go down to the lake and wash your face. We've got to be on our way." Maggie, struggling to get the knapsack up onto her back, was fast losing patience.

"Okay, okay," he mumbled. "You're worse than my mother."

Thankfully, it had not rained during the night, but the overhanging branches of the still sodden trees dripped endlessly on their heads as they trudged back along the narrow track.

"We would have been down the mountain by now if we'd taken the right road," Gordon said in an aggrieved voice as if taking the wrong one had been entirely Maggie's fault.

She refused to take the bait. "It was very dark if you remember, and we were both very tired. I'm sure we'll be back on the right road soon." But it was more than an hour before they returned to the place where they had last seen the bear, and in the daylight Maggie realized how easy it had been for them to take the wrong track as there was a maze of old logging roads branching off at that point. Now they took their time, carefully checking them all out before finding the one with recent tire tracks.

They were about to head down it when Maggie said, "Listen!" As they stood in silence, far below they could hear the faint sound of cars passing. Though hungry and exhausted, they started off again, almost running now.

"SO WHAT DO WE do now?" Fiona asked.

"We keep walking up that track until we find them," Nat said. "See those car tracks? There's two sets of them, so Maggie's car must have been driven farther up the mountain and then down again. Which means that Maggie and Gordon are up there somewhere. Come on, Oscar. Find Maggie!"

"AT LEAST WE'RE NOW on the right track, Gordon, and there's a highway down there somewhere."

"How can you tell with all these damn trees?" he answered miserably. The hillside was steeper here so the road wound back and forth, but it had been logged some years earlier and on either side of the track it was now thick with young jack pines and brush. "And what if that crazy old man comes after us . . .or the bear picks up our scent again?"

"Well," she answered as cheerfully as she could, "let's walk a bit faster then, shall we?" And she continued around the next bend in the road.

"Wait! Maggie, stop! There's something down there on the road."

"Where?"

"It's some kind of animal!" He pointed through the trees and down the steep incline. "See?"

Suddenly an exhausted, wet, muddy, furry creature rounded the bend in the track and flung itself at Maggie with yelps of delight and excitement. She sank to her knees, tears streaming down her face as she hugged Oscar to her. "Where's Nat, Oscar? Where's Nat?"

"Right here." Nat, very much out of breath, stumbled up the hill to where she was kneeling and, pulling her to her feet, wrapped his strong arms around her. "Oh, Maggie, my love, I've been so worried. Thank god you're safe!"

"Mum. It's my mum!" Gordon, crying, ran towards Fiona and the two of them were soon hugging. "I thought I'd never see you again. And I'm so hungry, and I just want to go home."

"Thank God, you're safe," Fiona said through her tears. "Thank God you're safe!" After a minute or two, still holding tight to her son, she walked over to Maggie. "Thank you," she said simply. "I know I've been a bitch. But you found him, just as you promised."

"Not so fast. Hand over me gun."

"Jesus! Who's that?" Nat exclaimed, staring at the apparition that had just appeared around the bend in the road above them.

Maggie sighed. She had known Gibbs would turn up sooner or later. "Let me introduce you to Mr. Livingstone Stanley Gibbs. He thought I'd make an excellent wife and tied me up to prove it."

"I'd keep away from that woman if I was you, mister," Gibbs yelled, taking a few steps closer. "She's a mean one. Hit me over the head with me fryin' pan, she did. Wonder she didn't kill me."

"You can give him back his gun now, Gordon," Maggie said. "I unloaded the shells before we set out this morning. And you, Mr. Gibbs, can expect a visit from the police. Kidnapping is a federal crime."

"Had a right, I did. Yer was trespassing on me propitty. And yer can tell them cops from me that if they come a-visiting, they'll git a bellyful of buckshot."

Just as he stepped forward to grab the gun, Nat said, "Hold it!" and took the gun from Gordon. "Empty your pockets, Gibbs!"

"Whatcha talking about?" Gibbs said, reaching for the gun again.

"I said empty your pockets," Nat repeated.

Slowly Gibbs fumbled in his coat pockets and hauled out a handful of shotgun shells.

Nat nodded to Gordon. "Go get them."

When Gordon had collected them, Nat slipped one of them into the gun and pointed it at Gibbs. "Now the rest of them, Gibbs."

"There ain't no more," Gibbs said. Nat waited, still pointing the gun, and finally Gibbs' hands began going from pocket to pocket, each time coming out with a few more shells.

When he figured they had them all, Nat said, "Okay, Gibbs, you can have your gun back." And he heaved it with all his strength into the dense young forest below them.

With a roar of anger and disbelief, Gibbs charged into the trees after it.

"Come on, Maggie," Nat said, "let's get you back to Bianca's."

"My car," she said. "Those thugs stole my car."

"It's just down the track. It's a bit scratched up, but I'm sure it's still drivable."

CHAPTER TWENTY-FIVE

A week later, Maggie now rested and well fed by Bianca, sat beside Nat in Sergeant Allen's office.

"I hear you will soon be returning to Vancouver, Mrs. Spencer. I'm sorry your vacation didn't turn out as you expected."

Maggie laughed. "You can say that again. But I hear you have arrested Major Stroud?"

"Huh! Some major. Our enquiries show that he had a very short military career before being dishonorably discharged for drug dealing and a long list of other misdemeanors."

"He seems to have carried the same bad habits into his private life," Nat commented.

"Especially the drug smuggling," the sergeant went on. "Buying the apple orchard was a stroke of genius on his part because his thugs could bring the drugs here from Central America disguised as casual labour."

"Very neat," Nat said. "They also acted as heavies whenever there was trouble, like when the Herrmanns were trying to put one over on him."

"Which, in turn, caused Adam Hermann's murder," Maggie said slowly. "What a terrible thing to happen. . ."

"Yes," the sergeant said. "We think the boy must have figured he could make some extra profit by holding out on them, probably not realizing they'd count the money right there before they let him set off with the drugs. I don't know if Fiona Phelps realizes how close Gordon was to being killed, too. I'm guessing they had no idea he was hiding in the vestry at the time."

"What about Peter Hermann?" Nat asked. "Did you manage to apprehend him?"

"Oh, yes. He still insists the money in the shed is legitimately his, but he couldn't give us a satisfactory explanation about where it came from. But he and his wife are very distraught over the death of their only son, which leads me to believe that one of them will crack soon and we'll get the truth."

"But what a price to pay," Maggie said sadly.

The sergeant nodded. "On a happier note, I hear you have your car back."

Maggie smiled. "Yes. It was covered in mud and badly scratched, but a fresh coat of paint and it's raring to go. Nat and I will be leaving for home in convoy tomorrow."

THE FOLLOWING MORNING A teary-eyed Bianca held Maggie close. "I'm going to miss you so. You seem like part of my family now, and we can't thank you enough for all you did to get to the truth on who really set the church on fire. I know that Carl Schultz feels greatly in your debt."

"He's already thanked me," Maggie said, smiling. "And he gave me these to keep me going on the road." She opened the brown paper bag she was carrying. "See, he made me some cinnamon buns. Bye, Bianca. I'll be back."

Bianca and Alonso Rinaldi waited until Maggie had climbed into her newly repainted red car and watched as she drove off closely followed by Nat in his old Chevy.

"She's in good hands," Alonso said, turning to go inside. "That Nat is one great guy."

CHAPTER TWENTY-SIX

Maggie breathed a sigh of relief as she parked her car at the rear of her small house on Fifth Avenue in Kitsilano. Nat had volunteered to help her unload her luggage and make her a cup of tea, but all she wanted was to be inside her very own place all by herself. Her cat, Emily, miffed at being left for so long, completely ignored her, and Maggie figured it would be a while before she was forgiven. But she wasn't too worried because Emily had been well looked after by her neighbour's teen-aged daughter who adored the finicky feline. Oscar was happy to be home, too, and forgetting Emily had sharp claws and wasn't too partial to the usurper dog, had rushed over to give her a sloppy lick. Chastened, he flopped into his familiar warm basket and slept.

Maggie bent and lit the prepared fire in the grate and waited a while for the room to warm up before lugging hcr suitcase up the stairs to her bedroom. The bed looked so inviting, but she resisted flinging herself onto it until she had unpacked and had stowed her clothes in the closet and dressing table. Both the animals needed to be fed, and although she and Nat had stopped for a very late lunch, she desperately needed a cup of her special blend of tea.

She awoke early the next morning to find Emily cuddled behind her knees and Oscar lying at her feet. She had been forgiven. Pushing the sleeping animals aside without disturbing them, she went downstairs to make coffee and collect the Saturday newspaper from her front porch. Ah, the luxury of one's own home. After breakfast she would grocery shop.

Two slices of French toast and maple syrup later she refilled her cup and began working her way through the accumulated pile of mail. Most of it was junk but there were a few bills that she set aside to deal with later. Pulling a notepad in front of her, she began to write her grocery list. She was so engrossed in this familiar ritual that it was a few minutes before she realized that the insistent ringing was her front door bell.

Who could it be on a Saturday? "Oh," she said aloud, "it must be the paper boy coming to collect. But how does he know I'm back? Okay, okay, I'm coming." Oscar roared down the stairs from the bedroom barking shrilly and reached the door first.

To her complete surprise, the hand on her brass knocker, ready to use it to thump the door for added emphasis, belonged to Harry, her estranged husband.

"What the hell. . . My God, it's you, Harry! What's wrong?" Naturally her first thoughts were for her family because why else would the man be standing there? "Is it one of the girls? Is the baby okay?"

"Calm down, Margaret. As far as I know, the girls and the children are fine. May I come in?"

Maggie stepped aside for Harry to enter, closed the door behind him and led him through to the kitchen.

"What is it, Harry? You seem a bit. . ." Her voice trailed off. He definitely looked different. "You're not ill, are you?"

"Margaret, do stop fussing. I am perfectly all right. No, I've come to ask you something." He looked around the room. "That man isn't here, I hope."

"If you mean Nat, no, he's not here."

"May I sit?"

Maggie nodded and indicated a chair at the kitchen table. "Would you like some coffee or tea?"

"Where have you been?" he asked, totally ignoring her offer. His hand automatically slid down to stroke the head of the traitorous Emily who simply adored Harry. "I've called you repeatedly on the telephone. I've called that place where you work, and that mad woman you employ absolutely refused to tell me where you were."

"I was on vacation in the Okanagan. Now what's so urgent?"

"It's about the divorce. I'm. . .uh. . . I've thought it over and I'm willing to grant you one."

"You're what?"

"I agree to the divorce."

Maggie grinned wickedly. "Don't tell me you've met somebody."

Harry actually blushed. It started from his correctly knotted Yale tie and slowly ran up his face. "Yes. I've no need to say more."

"Who is she?" Maggie persisted. "Do I know her?"

"Suffice it to say that I wish to keep her completely out of the proceedings. There is no reason for her to be dragged into something so. . . so unsavoury." He shuddered.

Poor Harry! Maggie thought. *What it must be costing him to be the one asking for a divorce.* "I find it a bit hard to understand, Harry. For the last four years you've been so reluctant to grant me one and now here you are. . ." She walked over to the stove and poured out two cups of coffee from the carafe and, after adding cream and sugar to one, placed it in front of him. "But you see, I've got used to living as I am. I don't feel any guilt for 'living in sin' as you label it. In fact, come to think of it, I'm no longer in any hurry to change my status."

He gaped at her. "Margaret, you can't mean that! You must agree. . . I'll even be willing to be the one found . . .uh. . .in flagrante delicto." He sipped his coffee.

Maggie grinned at her straight-laced husband. "You mean found doing it in a cheap hotel?"

"Margaret! There is no need to be so vulgar. You know perfectly well what I meant."

"I'll really have to think about it, Harry."

"I understand." He rose from the table. "You intend to be difficult. Please let me know as soon as possible, Margaret. My . . . uh . . . lady friend needs to plan for our . . . future." He walked to the door. "That reminds me. Please make a list of anything you would like from the house . . . within reason, of course."

"I can't think of a thing, Harry. Of course, the girls might like something." She opened the front door and watched him walk to where he'd parked his Chrysler Windsor. Although the car was at least five years old, it still had that fresh-from-the showroom look. She turned and walked back into the house.

"I must call Nat," she told Oscar.

"I was just about to call you," Nat said when he recognized her voice.

"Nat, you'll never guess who's just been to see me?"

"Midge?"

"No. Harry."

"Harry! What the hell does he want? More pleading for you to go back to him?"

"No, the opposite. He wants a divorce."

There was silence on the other end of the line, then Nat said, "You know, I have a funny hunch this has something to do with George's activities while we were gone."

"George! He doesn't know Harry. How could it have anything to do with him?"

"Is it okay if we come over?"

"Is this something to do with Harry?"

"George will explain when he sees you."

"Well. . .okay." Maggie replaced the receiver and realized that her plans for the day had taken an unusual turn. "George doesn't even know Harry," she told Oscar. And the dog, settling for a snooze in his basket, thumped his tail. She bent and stroked his head. "It's okay, Oscar. Everything's fine."

"So what's going on?" she asked when the two men arrived.

They removed their coats and made for the warm kitchen where George pulled out a chair and placed a thick notebook on the table. "Pour us some coffee, Maggie, and I'll do my best to explain."

"What's it about?"

"George has been very busy while we were both away," Nat said. He turned to his old pal. "For God's sake, man. Get on with it!"

"As I told Nat, I did a little extra surveillance while you were both in Naramata."

"You mean on that Sowerby fraud case?" Maggie asked. "So what did you find out?"

"No, not the Sowerby case, though I think we've resolved that one, too. But this is something I did on my own time." He tilted his head toward Nat. "You see, Nat and I had a little discussion about Harry's unwillingness to give you a divorce."

Nat nodded. "It was the weekend you left on your supposedly restful vacation, Maggie."

"That's correct. Well, you know how good I am at surveillance." He turned to explain to Maggie. "During our time on the force Nat and I worked on a number of stake-outs together, and we got pretty damned good at it, didn't we, Nat? And I was missing that, you see, so knowing how unhappy you've both been about this divorce business, I decided to use my skills for a little bit of off-duty tracking."

"You mean you tracked Harry?" Maggie asked, laughing. "He would never do anything clandestine. He's too. . .what's the word. . . upright to misbehave."

George grinned. "Believe me, Maggie, nobody is too upright to misbehave. So I started by following him to see what he did with his time when he wasn't in the office. I found him to be very consistent. He leaves his office precisely the same time each evening exactly thirty minutes after his secretary leaves."

"Miss Fitch-Smythe," Maggie said. "She's been his secretary for years and she absolutely loathes me."

George smiled. "I knew I was fairly safe in following him as the only time he's ever seen me was at Shadow Lake after Nat fell down that mine shaft."

"Of course," Maggie said. "The Chandler case."

"I figured he wouldn't recognize me again—different setting, different circumstances—and he didn't, so I was able to follow him quite easily. Tuesdays and Thursdays he went straight home but Mondays, Wednesdays and Fridays he drove over the Lions Gate Bridge to a hotel on the North Shore—usually the Grouse Inn."

"Whatever was he doing there?" Maggie asked.

"Meeting his lady love, of course."

"In a hotel room?" Maggie exploded. "Who is she? Do I know her?"

"Oh yes," George said, "you know her. It's Miss Amelia Fitch-Smythe."

"I don't believe it! His secretary!" Then Maggie laughed. "I never knew her name was Amelia."

"Did you follow them on weekends, too?" Nat asked. "I wouldn't think Lucille would have liked that."

"I only did it once on a weekend and Lucille came with me. We drove past your old address on Elm Street, Maggie. Harry was having tea with some people in the garden. I think it was one of your daughters and her family. It's a lovely house."

Maggie nodded. "Must have been Barbara, Charles and their two little ones. And yes, it is a lovely house. I have some beautiful memories of bringing up my girls there," she said sadly. "It just got intolerable after they left."

"What I can't understand," Nat said slowly, "is why he is offering you a divorce now."

"I think he twigged he was being followed the last time I went after him by myself. So that's when I enlisted Henny to help." And George then told them the whole story of Henny and her glass of soda with a twist of lemon, of her following Harry up to the fourth floor and discovering the room number. "But he must have recognized her because, while Henny and I were still in the carpark deciding what to do next, we saw them leaving—in quite a hurry." He grinned. "I was disappointed because I had planned to go up there and catch them in bed together, but if he's asking you for a divorce, it looks as if Henny's performance did the trick."

"Poor Harry," Maggie said. "He must have been so embarrassed. I've always known that Miss Fitch-Smythe had a thing for him, though I can't believe he's serious about marrying her." She looked down at her ring-less left hand. "But I wonder if my girls know anything about this?"

"So," Nat asked Maggie gently, "what was your answer to Harry?"

"I told him I'd got used to my lifestyle and that I would have to think about it."

"Do you really have to think about it?" he asked anxiously.

She got up from the table, and standing behind his chair, she wrapped her arms around him. "He's kept me waiting a long time, Nat. Now it's his turn to wait."

"But not for long, I hope."

She bent down and kissed his cheek.

IT WAS LATER THAT AFTERNOON. Nat and George had gone their separate ways—Nat back to the office and George home to enjoy the rest of the weekend with Lucille. Maggie, on the other hand, spent a couple of hours grocery shopping—and thinking. After returning home, she tried to put Harry and the divorce from her mind, but it was difficult to do. With the shopping put away and Emily and Oscar dozing, she was about to put the kettle on for tea when the doorbell rang.

Oh, dear God. Not Harry again.

"You're back at long last!" Barbara, her usually neat blonde hair in disarray, stormed past her mother and into the kitchen. "Where the hell have you been? I've tried repeatedly to reach you. Do you know Daddy wants to marry that. . .that. . . secretary of his? It's absolutely pre-posterous. You've got to put a stop to it." She sat down on the nearest chair and burst into tears. "And it's all your fault."

"My fault!" Even as she said the words, Maggie real-ized that in her daughter's eyes, it *was* all her fault. She sat down opposite her first-born and reached for her hands. "Barbara, he's a grown man. And he's probably a very lonely one. He needs a companion and I'm afraid I'm not it."

"But why not? You had a wonderful life with Daddy, Midge and me. Why did you have to spoil it by going to work for that. . . that detective? He's not even our sort of person."

"Barbara dear, Nat is very much my sort of person. He is a great part of my life. He has brought me joy, ex-citement and a reason for living. And I love him."

Barbara groped in her pocket for a handkerchief and mopped her eyes. "Do you realize what's it like for my children? Their grandfather lives in one house and you live in another."

Maggie got to her feet. "Would you like some tea?"

"No. It's no use talking to you. I'm going home."

Midge's phone call was totally different.

"I'm not too worried," she informed her mother. "At least you'll be free to marry Nat . . . that's if you want to. And as for Dad marrying Amelia Fitch-Smythe . . ." She paused. "I can't honestly see him taking that step—but if he does, then it's up to him."

After Midge hung up, Maggie sank into her easy chair, thankful to be on her own at last. What a year! Emily jumped into her lap and, purring contentedly, curled herself into a white fluffy ball. Oscar, leaning close to her chair, knew that a hand was near for the odd rub behind the ears.

She dearly loved Nat. But did she want to give up the pleasure of living on her own in her very own place? Perhaps Nat could be persuaded to carry on just as they were.

. .

About the Author

Gwendolyn Southin was born in Essex, England, but spent most of her married life in Montreal. She and her husband emigrated to Montreal, and in 1982 after retiring from their respective careers, they moved to the Sunshine Coast of BC where she finally embarked on the writing career she had always wanted. Her short stories and articles appeared in numerous journals and newspapers, and she became one of the "founding mothers" of the renowned Festival of the Written Arts, now in its 38th year. Her first book in the six-volume Margaret Spencer Mystery series, Death in the Family Way, was published in 2000. Gwen now lives in Victoria, BC, where in 2017 she was voted Amica Retirement Homes' "Inspiring Senior of the Year."